Birth of the CHOSEN ONE

ERICA TRANTHAM

NEWMAN SPRINGS PUBLISHING
320 Broad Street
Red Bank, NJ 07701

First originally published by Newman Springs Publishing 2021

ISBN 978-1-63692-762-6 (Paperback)
ISBN 978-1-63692-763-3 (Digital)

Printed in the United States of America

To Allyson

CHAPTER

I could feel my legs burning as I was running as fast as I could to get away from the big, horrible-smelling wolf. I did not know how much longer I could keep going. It is not like I am out of shape but just lazy. I could feel him breathing down on my hind legs. This is how I die. This is how my life ends. It has not been the best of life, but it was my life. See, my mom left me on the doorsteps on the fire station when I was only four weeks old. She did not want me but thought she could do it. But she was wrong. So I was taken to a home and was there for only three weeks before someone adopted me. That someone should have never had kids. The woman drank all day and did drugs. The man just sat on his butt all day drinking. However, on bad days, he would beat me to where he broke my bones. My ribs may never be the same again. I was sixteen when I ran away from that place. It was the night of my sixteenth birthday that my body began to pop and crack and got a fever. I ran out into the woods afraid of screaming and those people hearing me. That was when I learned that I am not human. I am not a vampire or a werewolf either. I am what is called a shape-shifter. I can change into anything I want.

Now back to the wolf chasing me. You see, I was in the form of a fox right now, and I went into their land and stole some food. They did not know that I was a girl as a fox, that I knew of. But then again, they could know and were chasing me to put me in their basement. Yikes!

I saw a big, rough-looking tree ahead of me and saw a small hole in it. So I started to run faster so the mean wolf did not catch me. I jumped with all my might and landed in that hole. The wolf jumped after me and got his snout stuck in the hole. I moved to the back of the tree as fast as I could and started to change shapes again. I thought of a spider. And next thing I knew, my fur was gone, and eight legs were now in the place of my four legs. The wolf kept scratching up against the tree trying to free himself. I just hung out watching him and laughing in my head.

He finally got himself free and looked into the hole with one eye. I have to say that was a very pretty eye of green. I have never seen an eye like that before, almost like moss going on a tree trunk. The wolf huffed and backed up. Next, I heard his bones popping and cracking. Next thing I knew, there was a man looking into the tree. He had the same eyes of the wolf, so I knew this was him. He looked to the left, to the right, up, and then down. He kept mumbling to himself to where I could not understand him. I am sure he was talking about me and trying to figure out where I went. I thought I would have a little fun with him, so when he put his face back up to the hole, I crawled onto his nose. Next thing I knew, he was screaming like a five-year-old girl slapping at me. I jumped down off him and crawled over to the roots of the tree. He started to look around for me and then started to thump his big feet down on the ground trying to kill anything in his way.

I crawled over to the other side of the tree and changed yet again, this time into a hummingbird, and started to fly around. He saw me and stopped what he was doing and just looked at me. I thought that I had had enough of playing with this wolf and just flew up into the sky and off to home. That was a fun afternoon, but so thankful I did not get eaten.

I got back to my run-down little shack and flew in through an open window. I landed on the floor and slowly started to change back into me. I lay on the floor for a little bit just breathing in and out. Changing that much took its toll out on me. Once I got my breathing back together, I got up and pulled my clothes back on. How about we take a step back and I tell you a little about me? My name is Willow Storm. I am eighteen years old and have been on my own since I was sixteen. I could not stay with those people who said they were my parents. I know they are not as they are humans and I am not. I tried to get a job, but without my paperwork, I could not. Those people still have it all. So I found this run-down old shack and made it my home. I steal the food I need, or I eat what I find on the land. I hate eating raw meat, but if I am in a tiger form, it is not so bad. People say I am short; and I guess at five feet, two inches, that is short. I have long brown hair that has a mind of its own. Some days, it is straight; some days, it is wavy. It cannot make up its mind. I have sky-blue eyes. On a good day, they look almost see-through. On a bad day, it looks like storms are moving in my eyes. I am of average weight, I guess. I am not skin and bones, but I am not curvy either. If I had my choice, I would eat all day and weigh more. I did not finish high school, but I have been taking books from the library to be able to get my GED.

My home is all run down. There are holes in the roof and windows broken. There is no heat or AC. But I have running water, so I am glad I do not have to wash in the river. That thing is cold and fast moving. My clothes all have holes in them—dirty and just dingy. If I could make some money, I would go buy new clothes. I have been wearing these for two years now. I must find work so I can get out of here and live the dream life.

Now as for my mate, I have never found him. I would love to find him, and then he would take care of me. Be a happy ever after. I wish I could have that life because this one is getting old. My so-called parents were horrible people. They would beat me on bad and good days. I was their slave. It was always do this and do that. I was never my own person. I could not have a door on my room, and my father would want to do checks on me to make sure I was not cutting myself or out with the boys, making money sleeping with them. Now do not think he would touch me in a sexual way because that was not the case. If he even looked at me wrong, my mother would pop him in the back of the head and yell at him. No one wanted to get on her bad side. Now I do not know if they are looking for me, and I really do not care. I do not want to go back, and I will do everything in my power to stay away.

This is the life of Willow, the poor girl who is getting ready to be on the run.

CHAPTER

I was walking down the street just looking in the windows wanting to get some food. But I did not have any money on me, and I knew I could not end up in jail. So I stepped off into the alley and got down on all fours and started to think of a puppy dog. They are little and cute, and people love them. I could feel the hair start to come out of my arms as I turned furry. I could feel my ears start to get longer while my nose got bigger. My spine started to snap, and a tail started to grow out. I closed my eyes not wanting to see the in-between stages. I fell to the ground as I fought to breathe. Slowly I took those breaths in and out to slow my heartbeat. Once I knew I was back to being me, I jumped out from the alley and started to walk back to the meat shop.

Man, I hope he will give me some cooked bacon today.

I got up to the old wooden door just as it opened. I looked up to see a man with tattoos from his neck into his shirt. If I looked closely enough, I could make them out under his white button-up. I looked down his chest and over to his arms. Those things were made huge, and more tattoos covered his arms and hands. I looked back up to his face to see him already looking at me with his head to the side. I looked into his blue eyes while he cocked his eyebrow.

"Hey, Jon! You got a cute little puppy at your door!" I heard him yell while still looking at me.

Jon came walking up to the door to look down at me. He smiled at me while patting this guy on his back.

"Yeah, this little girl comes here all the time begging for food. I feel so sorry for her and wish that I could just take her home with me, but Sally is allergic to dogs," Jon said while bending down to scratch behind my ear.

I yapped at him so he would know that I loved the attention that I was getting. The big guy bent down on one knee to look at me and to let me sniff him. I slowly moved forward to sniff him to see what he smelled like. I was able to smell coconuts and woods smell. He looked at me again with that cocked eyebrow and petted the top of my head.

"Man, she needs a bath and a good brushing. Do you know who she belongs to?" asked the man.

"No, sorry, Asher, I have no clue whom she belongs to, if anyone. I have seen her here for about two weeks now, and no one has put up missing posters."

So the big man's name is Asher. Asher looked at me a little bit more and then reached for me and picked me up. Right away, I felt warmth coming off him. I licked his arms, and he laughed at me.

"Well, look at that. She likes you," Jon said.

"I think I will take her home with me and give her a good bath and feed her. She doesn't need to be out on the streets in the cold and dark."

"I'm glad you are going to care for her. Maybe it is what you both need, someone there for the other."

Asher looked at Jon and gave a sigh and said, "Yeah, I guess you are right. This could be good for me."

Asher picked up his bag of food and waved bye to Jon and headed out the door. I was not sure about this, but to have a good bath and brush with food, I think I will take my chance. Asher walked over to a motorcycle and put the bag down on the ground. He looked at me and smiled while he tucked me into a bag on the side of the seat. Next, he put the bag of food into the sack on the other side. He told me to sit tight and we would be home fast. I was shaking as I have never been on a motorcycle and never as a dog where I could not hang on. Asher patted my head as he started up the cycle, and off we went. At first, I tucked my head into the bag as I was scared. But as time went on, I gently pulled my head up to see the world around me.

The trees were going by so fast that it was hard to make them out. I watched as we went around the bend that I could see the river to the right of us. If I looked close enough, I could see my shack as we went by. But then I thought it was all in my head since the trees were hard to make out. The bike started to slow down, and I looked up to see why we were going slower. Asher made a turn to the right and started to go down a dirt road. I kept looking out over the river to see if I really saw my shack, and there it was, sitting all by itself. Asher came to a stop and looked over to see what I was looking at.

Asher laughed and told me that was his hunting cabin that he forgot to keep up, that he knew someone is living in it now but he did not care, and that he thought that person was taking good care of it. I smiled at him and felt good about myself. Asher started the bike back up and went a little farther down this road and came to a stop in front of another cabin. I was just sitting here in this bag on the side of his bike with my little jaw hung open. Asher laughed at me while patting my head.

"Yeah, it isn't much, but to me, it is home."

I could not believe my ears; this was not much? It looked like heaven. He had a roof that did not look like it had any holes in it. He had windows that were not broken. He had a door that half of it was not missing. To me, this was heaven. Asher came over and picked me up out of the bag and then got his bag of food and headed up the wooden porch steps. He came to the oak door and set the bag down so he can open the door. After the door was opened and we entered, he closed the door so I would not run away. He set me down on the floor and told me not to pee on his floors. Like I would be that stupid to mess this up. He went through another door, so I followed him and saw that it was his kitchen. I looked around, and everything was made from wood. I was guessing oak or pine. He had an incredibly old-looking wood table with one chair at it. I looked back at him, and he was emptying the bag into the fridge. So, I stepped out of the room and went to the living room to have a look around.

He had old furniture and more wooden tables and shelves in here. He had a big-screen TV on the wall above the fireplace. There were a ton of movies and books on the shelves and a big light on the wooden table with some empty beer bottles. Seeing those made me worry that he was going to hit me like my so-called parents did. Asher came walking into the room and saw me looking at the bottles.

"Do not worry, little one. Those were from my friends coming over last night. I just have not cleaned up yet. I do not drink. No reason to be afraid of me."

I let out a breath I did not know I was even holding in.

Asher laughed at me and said, "I thought you looked like you were getting hit by your last owners. I am also guessing that they drank. Do not worry. I got you."

Asher came over and picked me up and made his way to the back of the cabin. We passed three closed doors along the way. He came to the last room and flipped on the light. I looked around, and it was a black-and-white tile floor with white walls. He had a big clawfoot tub with a big sink against the other wall. The toilet looked too small for his big body. That got me to thinking how he got this big. Did he eat some little dude? He must have worked out night and day as I could see his veins popping out.

Asher walked over to the tub and turned the water on and let it warm up before he put the stopper in. He walked over and closed the door thinking I was going to run. Yeah, that was not happening. I needed this bath. When the tub had a little water in it, he turned off the water and picked me up. I licked his face as he passed it and laughed at me. He set me in the water, and I lay down on my belly before rolling all around.

"Well, I do not have to worry about you not liking a bath. How about we get you cleaned up now? I don't have puppy shampoo, so mine will have to work."

I watched him with half my face underwater. He squeezed some onto his hand, and I lifted my nose out of the water to smell. That is the coconut smell. He rubbed some on my head and then started to work his way down. I felt like I was a big bubble with as much of a lather he gave me. He worked it down my front legs and to my paws and then the same with my back legs. He got my tail and then stopped himself and looked at me again. I just tilted my head to the side as like to ask him what.

He took a deep breath and then said, "I know you are a dog, but I am having a hard time washing your girl parts."

I got so tickled as I saw him blush. So being the good girl dog that I am, I rolled around in the tub getting soap down to that area and then rubbed my front paw on that area. He looked at me with his eyes wide open and his mouth on the floor. I looked up at him and gave him a puppy smile. He shook his head and just laughed at me.

"Sometimes I think you know what I am saying, which is weird 'cause I have never met a puppy wolf before. Wolves do not change until they are eighteen."

I sat there looking at him, thinking, *Crap, I found a werewolf.* I just got rid of one, and now I found another one. Asher got done washing and rinsing me that he pulled the stopper and went to get a towel. I was jumping around in the water playing and chasing the bubbles down the drain. I heard him let out a belly-shaking laugh and stopped and looked up at him with wide eyes.

"Oh, that was great, little one. I have not laughed like that in years. Thank you. Maybe Jon is right. We need each other."

Asher picked me up and started to dry me while I licked his face over and over. I thought I might have found my new home. Once I was dry, he took me into the living room and pulled out a brush. I lay down on his lap and just let him work all the knots out. This was heaven. I could fall asleep right now if it were not for my tummy talking. Asher picked me up and took me into the kitchen and set me down on the ground. He walked to the fridge to pull something out. I was way too short to see what he got out. He walked over to the stove and pulled out a skillet. He then went to the cabinet and pulled out a bowl and filled it with water before putting it in front of me. I smelled it first, like a puppy would, and then started to drink the whole bowl dry. Yum, that was good. I then smelled meat being cooked and hoped I would get some of it.

Asher walked over to the cabinet again and pulled out a plate and then got a fork and knife. I knew then I was not getting any of it. I watched him place a big steak onto the plate and then go and sit at the table. Like a good puppy, I sat on the floor just watching every move he made. He sat down and cut the first bite off and popped it into his mouth. Oh man, I wanted to bite into it. He closed his eyes and chewed for a little bit before he swallowed it down. Next, he cut off another bite and looked at me. I just kept looking at him without moving from my spot. I had no clue why he was looking at me like that. Then he tossed the bite at me, and I jumped and caught it in the air. I, too, closed my eyes as the taste exploded on my tongue.

Oh, he is a great cook.

I heard him laughing at me as he took his next bite. Together he and I shared the steak with me catching the bites in the air. After we were done with our food, he put a rope around my neck. I figured he was tying me up outside, but I was wrong. We walked around for a little bit while I peed here and there on things, and then we went back inside.

He pulled the rope off my neck and told me, "Let's go to bed."

I followed him down the hall again until we came to the second door, and he opened it, turning on the light. I looked around his room. He had a big bed made from wood in the middle of the room. Off to the left, there was a dresser; and to the right, a door which I figured was the closet. Asher took his shirt off and then his pants and was in nothing but his boxers. My little puppy face looked away while blushing. I heard Asher laugh a little and looked back at him.

"Are you really blushing? You are just a puppy, so why would you blush?"

I had to look away to get myself under control. I have never seen a six-pack before. I looked back at him, and he said that maybe he did not see what he thought he was seeing. He walked up to me and picked me up again. I just could not help it and had to lick his chest. He laid me on the bed then went to the door and closed it while flipping off the light. He crawled under the covers and pulled me to him while rubbing behind my ear. That is how I fell asleep.

CHAPTER

3

A week had passed with me being a puppy and living with Asher. It was not bad per se, but living as a puppy sucked. I was tired of peeing outside and doing other things outside. No girl should have to do that. But my tummy was so full that I think I might roll away soon. Right now, Asher was at work, and I was just lying on the couch. I had no idea what time he would get back, so I did not want to become human and have him catch me. As my eyes got heavy, I heard the door open. I looked up and saw Asher there talking with some other guys. He looked at me and smiled while walking into the room. I jumped up and ran to him, yapping my happy bark. Asher got down on his knee to scratch behind my ear while saying hi to me.

Asher stood up and walked into the door with four other guys following him. I could smell the werewolf on these guys and started to worry that they could smell me too. The first guy was of medium build and had brown hair and eyes. The second guy was tall and built. He had blue eyes and hair. The third guy was limping a little bit and was smaller. He had blue eyes and blond hair. The last guy came walking in, and I felt my back get tight as my breath came out in small bursts. It was the guy from the tree when I was a fox. He was looking at me with those mossy-green eyes with one eyebrow cocked up.

Asher came walking back into the living room with four beers and a water for himself. Right then and there, I wanted to go hide somewhere that was not in this room. Asher told everyone to have a seat and started to talk to his buddies. The fourth guy just kept looking at me. I got onto my tummy and started to army crawl out of the room. Out of sight, out of mind, right? I did not even make it to the other side of the room before I heard Asher's voice.

"Hey, little puppy, why don't you come sit here? You do not have to hide from us. No one here is going to hurt you. These are my best mates."

I looked from Asher to the other four guys, not sure what to do. I did not want them to smell me and know that I was not a real puppy.

How can I get out of this? Oh, I know. I need to pee.

So I walked over to Asher and started to whimper and look at the door.

"Oh, crap! I forgot! Here, little one, let me take you out," Asher said as he got up to get the rope, so I did not run off.

Right now, I wished he would forget that rope so I could run away. I started to the back door when I heard a very deep, gruff voice.

"Hey, I will do it for you. You have been working all day. Sit and take a break."

I looked over, and it was that fourth guy that kept looking at me.

Oh, no, not that.

"Okay, thanks. Sitting does feel good," Asher said. "Thanks, Eric."

Well, now I know the fourth guy's name.

Eric got up and walked up to me and grabbed the rope and started to lead me out the door. I slowly followed him out and started to smell around for a place to pee.

"Okay, cut the crap and change back into your human form. I need to talk to you," Eric said.

Oh no!

I just sat there looking at him like I did not know what he said.

"I know you are the fox that stole from me. Then you turned into that spider, and now you are a puppy staying at my friend's house. Give it up."

Well, I guessed there was no point in keeping this going. But I did not want to be naked in front of him. I looked up at him and shook my head and then bit at his pants.

"Oh, so you don't want to be naked in front of me. Okay, hold on. I got you."

So he tied me to a tree and went back inside. I started to gnaw on the rope hoping to free myself. I heard the door open while I was only halfway through the rope. Yup, not going to happen. Eric threw a shirt that was huge, then he turned around. I started to think of my human self, and I could feel my bones moving back into place and felt my fur get sucked back into my skin. I grabbed the shirt and put it on and then just stood there.

Eric turned his head to look at me and see if I was dressed yet. I was standing there with my head down facing the ground. I felt his body heat before I saw his feet. Next, I knew he was putting his finger under my chin and lifting my head up. I looked into his eyes and him just looking all over my face.

"My word, child. How old are you?"

"I'm eighteen. I am sorry. I did not mean to cause a problem with your friend. I was at the meat shop to get some hand-me-outs, and your friend took me home. I did not mean to stay here longer, but Asher has been so good to me that I did not want to leave."

Eric looked at me with sad eyes. "Now, you stole from me. You are living as a freeloader on my friend. What do you have to say for yourself?"

"I will say I'm sorry, and then I will move on to another area of my life. I just liked having a family," I said.

"What do you mean? You are just so young," Eric asked while looking at me with worry.

So I told him about my parents and how they treated me. I told him about being on the run and trying to make it on my own. He just looked at me like I kicked his wolf. It was sad to see this big-built guy looking so sad.

"Well, you need to go in and tell Asher what is going on and who you really are. I cannot let you be taken care of without him knowing the truth."

I hung my head, not wanting to do this. He was going to be so mad at me. So we turned and walked into the back door. All the guys were already in the kitchen cooking up some stir fry and drinking.

Everyone stopped what they were doing and just stood there looking at us two.

"What is going on, Eric?" asked Asher.

Eric nudged me to open my mouth and talk. I looked up at him with eyes that was begging for help. Eric let out a sigh before he turned to Asher to speak.

"Your puppy is not a real puppy. She is a shape-shifter, and she is standing right here."

Asher looked at me like he was begging me to deny what Eric had said.

"I am sorry, Asher. But what Eric has said is right. I am a shape-shifter, and I was looking for food from that meat store. I go there every other week to get food from that nice older man. I did not think he would ask you to take me home or for you to keep me. I thought a bath and food, and then I would be on my way. Another thing is that it is me that has been living in your old shack." I stood there with my face to the floor again, not wanting to look at him in the eyes.

"What is your name?" I heard Eric ask.

"Willow."

"Willow, let's go talk in the other room while these guys finish up dinner and get you something more to wear."

I turned on my heel and followed Asher into the bedroom. I watched him go over to his dresser and pulled out a pair of shorts with a drawstring. He handed them to me, and I just stood there holding them in my hands. They were soft and a dark-green color.

"Please put those on so I can stop looking at your legs." I heard Asher say.

I bent over and slipped them up my slender, tanned legs. I pulled the strings as far as they could go and knotted them. I stood there not saying anything nor looking up from the floor. He really needed to vacuum. I had left hair everywhere.

"Please look at me, Willow. I am not mad. I'm upset that I lost my puppy but not upset at you."

I looked up at Asher and let out a small smile. He just stood there looking at me for a little bit before he started to speak again.

"So you are the one living in my shack? How did you find it? Why are you there? What is going on? Please talk to me. I would like to understand."

I looked up at him and let out a sigh. "My parents are not my parents. I am adopted. They would drink all day and do drugs. They started to hit me and beat me, so I ran away. I am eighteen and cannot work because they still have everything. So I am on my own trying to survive."

He let out a big breath and looked at me with sad eyes. He told me that we would work on my shack and fix it up and get me a job. But for right now, I will be staying in his spare room. I was excited that I would still have a roof over my head and food in my tummy.

We walked back out into the kitchen to see that dinner was done. Everyone looked up at us and waited for Asher to say something.

"Guys, I would like you to meet Willow, who used to be my puppy. Willow, this is Eric, Mike, David, and Jason. Come have a seat and eat with us."

I sat down, and everyone started to talk and ask me questions—who was I, where I was from, who my family is, and why I am on my own. Things like that. It was a nice dinner, and after it was over, I got up to do the dishes. Eric came walking over to me and handed me his plate.

"I hope I did not get you into trouble, but I hate people taking advantage of my friends. I hope you understand," he said to me.

"Oh, yes, it is all good. Asher is going to be helping me out for a little while, and hopefully, I will be able to be on my own again soon. Thank you for helping me tell him because I was feeling bad about it."

Eric nodded his head and then turned to walk out. The rest of the night, the guys drank, and I sat on the back-porch steps looking up at the stars. I heard the back door open after about an hour, and Asher walked out.

"Everyone has left. You can come in now, and we will get that room set up for you," Asher said.

So I followed him inside and went to the room. It had dark wooden bed and tables with a dresser. We changed the bedding and got me a change of clothes. I went to the bathroom and took a fast shower using the same coconut shampoo. Once I was done, I changed into a new shirt and walked out brushing my hair. I came to my room and saw Asher sitting on the bed holding a picture.

"You okay, Asher?"

"Yeah, I am. Just sleep tight and have a good night." He took the picture and walked out of the room.

I crawled under the big blanket and sunk into the soft bed. *This is the life.* I closed my eyes and fell into a dreamless sleep.

CHAPTER

It had been a week since Asher found out about me. He was true to his word and got me a job as a waitress at the bar he works for. We had been working on the roof of the shack in our free time. It was a Friday night, and I was not looking forward to working with all those big werewolves. I had to wear skintight jeans and a low-cut tank top. Lucky for me, I got to wear tennis shoes since I would be walking everywhere tonight.

Asher told me we were leaving in five minutes, so I had to move my lazy butt faster. At six minutes, I walked to the front door.

"About time you got out here. What took you so long?"

"I'm sorry, but my hair would not go into the ponytail."

Asher just shook his head at me and walked out to the motorcycle. He hopped on and then told me to get on. I wished I were a puppy right now because I loved riding that way. This way, I had to hold on to Asher's stomach and feel his six-pack. I knew he was not my mate, but I really wished he were. He had been a rock to me, and I did not think I would have lasted this long without him. The drive was fast, and he told me I could get off now. I opened my eyes and looked around. Yeah, that was a fast ride.

We walked inside together, and all the girls who work here started to glare at me while eye-raping Asher. Poor guy did not even notice the way they looked at him. We walked over to the bar to put our stuff behind it, and I grabbed my apron for the night. It was already packed when we got in there. This was going to be a long night.

About halfway through the night, I was grabbed by a guy who was double my height. I stopped in my tracks afraid of what he was going to try.

"Hey, sugar, how about you sit on my lap while I drink my beer, and then you can go fetch me another one?"

I looked up at him, afraid of what to say or do. I did not want to make this man mad, as big as he was.

"I cannot do that, sir. I have to help all these other people."

He turned me around and placed me on his lap. I started to fight him and tried to get up. Next thing I knew, I was pulled off from this guy and placed behind a guy's back.

"I do not know who raised you, but that is not how we treat ladies."

I looked up to see the back head of this guy. He had long black hair pulled into a ponytail. I could see tattoos running up his arms and on his neck. I could not see over his shoulder, as big as he was. Were all of these guys this big? Did they drink a lot of milk to get to be giants?

The guy took a step back, taking me with him. The man who grabbed me stood up ready to fight him.

"That will not be smart, man," the big guy protecting me said.

"Oh, this is going to be fun. I'm going to kick your ass and then take her home with me."

I started to shake, afraid of what would happen if he was able to take me home. The protector guy pushed me away and told me to get out of the way as he swung at the gross guy. I ran over to the bar to tell the boss what was going on, but he was already walking over there.

"There will be no fighting in this bar and no touching other people the way that you just did," the boss said.

I just stood there watching and waiting for what will happen next. The big gross guy took a swing at the boss and kicked at the protector. Both the men grabbed him by his arms and pulled them behind him. They pushed him to the floor and told him to calm down. The gross guy started to snap and pop, and right then and there, I knew he was changing into his wolf. He kept his eyes on me for the first half of the change, and I jumped behind the bar. No way was he taking me. Asher came running over to me and kneeled.

"You have got to change right now. Something small so he cannot find you, and maybe fit into my pocket. But not a snake."

I smiled at the snake thing and then thought of a mouse. It had a furry little face and long tail. My body started to pop and crack while I blocked out everything else that was going on. After I changed, I was lying inside of my shirt trying to find my way out. I felt two hands grab me and lift me up. I looked up and saw it was Asher who took me. He started to pet me and rubbed his scent onto me and then placed me in his front pocket of his white button-up shirt. He stood up and made his way to the front door. He stopped at the door, and his eyes glazed over. I knew he was talking to someone but was not sure who.

Asher got on to his motorcycle and took off down the road with me still in his pocket. I was not sure where we were going. We came to a stop, and I looked out of his pocket. We were in the middle of the woods by a river. He took me out of his pocket and walked over to the river. He kneeled and started to run water over the back of me and all over my tummy. I started to shake because of the ice-cold water. When he was done, he pulled me into his chest and wrapped me up in a small hand towel that he carried on his cycle. He started to rub my little body, trying to warm me up. He then set me down on the ground, then walked back to his cycle, and grabbed something. When he turned around, I saw it was my clothes. He laid them next to me and told me to change back. After a little bit, I was able to change back. I picked up my clothes and put them on me.

"Why did you wash me?" I asked with my teeth chattering.

Asher looked at me, then walked over to me, and wrapped his arms around me, pulling me close to his chest. I could just melt into his warmth. He looked down at me and talked very softly to me like he was afraid I was going to fear him.

"I wanted to wash his scent off you. I could still smell it with mine. He can track you with that scent."

"Thank you for saving me, Asher."

He looked down at me and told me I was welcome, but we had to get this guy's scent from me before we went any farther. I was not sure how to do that. I did not even know I smelled like the guy. Asher had been hugging me and had me in his pocket, so how could his scent still be on me?

"Asher, how is that guy's scent still on me?"

"He is a tacker, and they can give off a scent that will attach to another person so they can find them later." He looked at me with sad eyes, not sure what to do.

"What do we do?" I asked him.

He let out a breath and told me I was not going to like what must be done. I just stood there in his warm arms waiting for him to tell me.

"I have to give you my scent that will last for a month." He let out a sigh after saying that. "I have to bite you on your leg by your downstairs, like a love bite."

I looked at him with big eyes and tried to back away from him, but he held me tight. Asher took a deep breath before speaking again.

"I promise that it is not sexual when I bite you. No matter how much I like you, I will not take away from your mate. This must be done here so that your scent stays here and he thinks that you jumped into the river. That is the only way he will leave you alone."

I took a deep breath and nodded my head. I pulled my pants down to my knees and lay down on the ground. I had never done anything like this, and I was afraid he would hurt me. I heard him sigh yet again before he got down next to me.

"I'm sorry, Willow. This will hurt a little bit because I have to sink my teeth into your thigh."

I held my breath and waited for him to bite me. It seemed like hours when it was only about five minutes before he came closer to me and wrapped his arm around me. He pulled me closer to him as he lowered his head to my thigh. He spread my legs apart, and I heard him sniff me. I was starting to get turned on. This was the guy that I wished was my mate, and he was getting ready to bite my leg. I held my breath as I felt his warm breath on my leg.

I felt something wet on my leg and looked down to see his eyes were closed and he was licking my leg, like he was tasting me before he would bite into me. When he opened his eyes, they were no longer the blue I love but a pure black. His wolf had now taken over his body, and that worried me. He then sniffed me again and let out a groan. Oh my gosh, that was hot! I knew he could smell me getting aroused. I could not help it. He closed his eyes again and lowered his head back down and licked the inside of my leg while he dug his hand into my thigh. Next, I felt his teeth sink into my leg.

I let out a scream because it was burning so bad. After about a minute, it turned into pleasure. I started to moan while he held me down and was still biting me. My back arched off the ground, and I ran my fingers through his hair. I wanted this man, and I wanted him now. I let out the loudest moan I had ever let out while I felt his finger graze my core. It was hot to the touch but oh so soft. I finally put my back on the ground and looked down at Asher. He was licking my leg now to close the wound. He looked up at me while having his tongue on me, and I could see that his eyes went back to the blue I love so much. His hands finally loosened up on me to where I could move. I watched him while I just lay there catching my breath. He stood up and turned away amazingly fast, but I could still see that he was rock hard. So he enjoyed it just as much as I did.

I stood up and pulled my pants up which stung at first. He did not face me while telling me that we needed to go before that guy showed up and that we have been here too long. I hopped onto the motorcycle after he got on and wrapped my arms around his waist. I heard Asher let out a groan, and I knew that I was affecting him now. The cycle started, and we headed back to the road and took off to home. I could feel my bite rubbing on my pants while we bounced around. I moaned while we took a turn and grabbed Asher tighter. He almost lost control and took a deep breath. Maybe we would not make it home safe after what just happened. What was I going to say to him when we would get there? How was it going to be between us now? Would he get protective of me? Well, he already protected me, but maybe it would be worse.

CHAPTER

We got back to the house, and I went to take a shower to cool my skin down from what happened at the river. I could not believe that I enjoyed that so much. I turned on the water to lukewarm so I could work my way down to cold water. I took off my clothes and stepped into the shower. I placed my head under the water with it rolling down my back. I closed my eyes and just rested my head on the shower wall. Flashes of what happened kept playing in my head, making me even hotter. I had to turn the water down to try to make it cooler. I grabbed the shampoo and washed my hair and then rinsed it out. I grabbed the soap to wash my body and started to rub it into my skin, slowly moving my hands downward while thinking about Asher and him biting me. I made it to my thigh and touched the bite mark, which made me moan out his name. I stopped and listened to see if he heard me. When I did not hear anything, I moved back to touching the bite mark, making me get more and more aroused. I heard Asher knock on the door.

"Willow! I swear you better stop that before I come in there and finish what happened!" he yelled through the door.

Did I want him to come in here and give him what was for my mate? Would I ever find my mate? Maybe I could make Asher my mate and not worry about finding whoever he is.

"Willow, stop it right now!" I barely heard him yell at me.

The shower curtain was ripped back, and there stood Asher in just his boxers looking at me with black eyes. His wolf had taken him over and wanted to finish what he had started, but Asher was also there because he still had on his boxers. Asher stepped into the shower and pinned me to the wall with the water running down the both of us. He placed his hands on the wall beside my head. I was holding my breath, not sure if I wanted this or not. I also was not sure if would be good enough for him.

Asher opened his eyes, and I saw the blue that I love so much. Asher was back.

"Willow, I am fighting to not take you right now. I am fighting not to finish what I started and make you my mate. There is not much left in me after I smelled you and tasted you. You have to tell me right now, right here, what you want."

I looked up into his eyes while my shaky hand ran up his wet six-pack to his neck. I grabbed him and pulled him down to me locking my lips with his. This was my first kiss, and I was afraid I was doing it wrong. He pulled back, breathing hard while looking into my eyes.

"As much as I want this, I cannot do that to you. I am not going to force you into this just because of a bite."

He then kissed my forehead and then stepped out of the shower, leaving me all hot and bothered.

Great, now I must make the shower ice cold.

*****

After five days, I was still thinking about that bite. Asher had been trying to avoid me and made me start thinking that my kiss was horrible and he did not want someone so innocent. I just kept working on the roof and working at the bar. That gross guy had not been back, so I was glad for that. We were at work again when I started to feel hot. I tried to cool down with some ice on my neck, but it was not helping. I noticed that a lot of the guys were looking at me and smelling the air.

What is going on?

I went over to a guy to take his drink order when his eyes started to go from brown to black. They kept going back and forth. I asked him what he wanted, and he just growled at me. I was worried I did something wrong, so I backed up and walked back to the bar.

"Hey, boss man, I tried to take that guy's order, but he just growled at me. Can someone else go over there?"

Boss man sniffed the air while his eyes also started going back and forth.

What the heck is going on here tonight?

I started to step back when I saw boss man's eyes went hazy.

Okay, he is talking to someone, but who?

I did not have to wait long before Asher was by my side also sniffing the air. He placed his hand on my forehead, and I moaned a little as his touch cooled me down.

Asher looked at boss man and said, "We are leaving. We will be back in a week. This is my fault, and I cannot leave her alone."

Boss man said okay and to get out fast. I did not know what the big deal was until Asher grabbed my hand to lead me out and all the men started to growl louder. Asher looked back at me and told me to run. So I ran following him to his motorcycle. I looked back and saw several of the men following us out. Asher cussed under his breath while turning into his wolf in the middle of a step. I had never seen someone change that fast. He was huge and pure black. We were shoulder to shoulder standing next to each other. I turned around to see what was going to happen. Asher bent over and growled at the other wolves. I knew this meant trouble, but I did not know why. What did I do?

Asher nudge me with his front leg and turned his head to push me on my butt. I raised an eyebrow at him, not understanding what he wanted. He rolled his wolf eyes at me and then got lower to the ground. I finally got what he was saying and climbed up onto his back. The cooling touch of him made me moan again. The wolves started to come closer, and Asher growled and turned to run as fast as he could. I lay down on him, holding on while my body bounced up and down. This was not good because I was getting aroused all over again. I was going to be a mess by the time we got home.

We got back home faster than I thought. Asher slowed down to a stop and bent down for me to climb off. I had shaky legs because I had never gone that fast through the woods. He started to snap and pop his bones back into place. I ran inside to get him a pair of shorts so he was not walking around naked. That was the last thing I needed to see right now. I closed my eyes and held my hand out with the shorts in my palm. I felt them being taken and then heard him say it was okay now. So I opened my eyes and looked at him. I felt him take my hand and lead me into the house, to the living room. He set me down on the couch and started to move back and forth while talking under his breath.

Finally, he stopped and looked at me with eyes changing from blue to black. He closed his eyes and took deep breaths trying to slow his heartbeat. After a while, he opened his eyes and looked at me with blue eyes.

"I'm sorry. I did not know, when I bit you, you would go into heat. There is not much I can do right now but have skin-to-skin to cool down your fever. But the only way to get rid of it fully is to mate with me. I have never seen anyone going into heat this fast or from a love bite like that one. I did not claim you as my mate, so I don't know what is going on." After he was done talking, he hung his head to the floor.

I sat there for a minute just taking in what he said. I was in heat. He put me in heat by the bite. He did not know why or how this happened. He had never seen it before. Fully mate. Skin-to-skin to cool me down. I looked up at Asher and asked him how long it would last.

"Five days is the normal length for heat. But this is all new, so I'm not sure what is going on or how long it will last." Then he walked off to another room down the hall.

I just sat there trying to figure it all out. I did not have a wolf like he does to ask what was going on. I had no one in my head like he does.

After about ten minutes, I got up and walked down the hall trying to find Asher. I saw him sitting on his bed with his eyes hazed over. I wondered whom he was talking to at a time like this.

Why is this more important than me and my heat?

I could feel my fever getting higher the madder I got. I could almost see the smoke coming off my arms while I made a fist. Asher jumped up off the bed fast and grabbed me into his arms. I fought him at first, but the cooling of his skin made me stop.

"I'm sorry. Please do not be mad at me. I was talking to our elder to see if he has heard of this and what can be done about it. Please calm down."

I took a deep breath and let it out slowly, trying to calm my heart and my head. I get why he was like that on the bed. But my body just would not stop shaking and getting hot. Asher felt that I was not calming down, so he picked me up and took me to the bathroom. He set me down on the ground while he turned the shower on and then picked me up and put into ice-cold water.

Holy mother, that is cold.

He climbed in behind me and started to pull my shirt off. I just stood there looking at him. He took a deep breath before he started to pull my jeans off. They rolled slowly down my legs. I stepped out of them, while Asher threw them somewhere else. I was standing there in my bra and panties while he was standing there in basketball shorts.

I looked up at Asher's eyes to see what color they were. They were this deepest blue I have ever seen. I really loved this color. It was like the ocean when a storm rolls in. I took a step closer to Asher one step at a time without breaking eye contact. He just stood there and let me come to him. He was breathing hard and deep. I got up to him and slid my fingertips up his arm to his shoulder. His body shook, and the hair rose up just by that little touch. I slid my fingers into his hair and pulled him closer to me as I smashed my lips onto his soft, strong ones. I felt Asher's arm come around my waist while he pulled me up against his body. I moaned into his mouth just feeling his skin on my skin. He held me for a little while before he started to wash my hair. I loved feeling his fingers rub my scalp. He turned me around so he could rinse my hair out. All the little hairs were now standing upright. It felt oh so good. He then turned me around again before grabbing the bar of soap. He worked it in his hands until it was all bubbly. He then started at my shoulders working his way down, missing what was under my bra and pantie. He then turned me again to rinse me off. I was sad that he did not wash me where I wanted him to touch me the most.

Asher looked at me from over my shoulder before kissing me on my ear. I felt my panties being lowered down my hips, down my legs, then off each foot before they were tossed somewhere else. He picked up the bar of soap again and worked it in his hands. He turned me again, so I was facing the wall with him behind me. I felt the heat of him behind me as he stepped closer to me. I wanted to lean back into him but fought it for now. His hands started at my belly button working in a circle as it moved lower and lower. I felt him kiss my ear as I moaned at the feel of his hands.

"It's okay, Willow. I'm going to take care of you now."

I did not know what he was talking about. My heat? Forever care for me? And then I felt his hand encounter my swollen nub. Slowly he started to add pressure while going around in a circle while I fell back into his chest. His other hand wrapped around my tummy to hold me to him while the circle became harder. I had never felt anything like this, and I never wanted it to stop. Asher started to move his finger slowly up and down my wet folds while I moaned. He slid one finger into me, moving at a slow speed. I needed him to go fast. I needed more. I laid my head back onto his shoulder and turned my head to face him while I placed a kiss on his cheek.

"Hold on, Willow. I got you" was all I heard before he drove his finger deep and hard into me. I stood up on my tippy toes from the force of it. He pulled his finger back out and added a second one in before he slammed into me again. Holly hell. He was pumping his finger into me hard and fast, making me moan and call out his name all the while my body was rubbing up against him. I heard him groan as my body came back down and felt his hard-on. I moved my hand behind me between us and grabbed his manhood. I started to rub him to the same speed he was fingering me. It was hard and fast, and I loved every moment of it while I moaned out his name. His hand slowly made its way up my body and into my bra to pinch my hard nipples. I did not think I could take much more now than he added that to the mix.

I heard his deep, husky voice next to my ear, "Come with me, little one."

And that was all it took as I hit my peak. I felt myself let go of the knot in my tummy and soaked his fingers with my juices. I felt hot liquid hit my back as he let out a loud moan saying my name. We stood there holding each other for a few moments before he let me go and started to wash my back off. I cleaned up my front area while he cleaned up himself. He turned off the shower and grabbed two towels. He wrapped one around me while he dried himself off. Then he tied the towel around his waist. He then came to me and started to dry me off. I loved the feel of his hands working the towel around my body and let out another moan. Asher picked me up, bridal style, and carried me back to his room. He set me down on the edge of the bed and walked to the closet. He came back with one of his T-shirts and placed it over my head, pulling my arms through. He then picked me back up and put into his bed. He went back to the closet and came out wearing just boxers. Yummy six-pack. He climbed under the blankets and pulled me close to him, so I could feel his skin.

"Good night, Willow. Sleep well."

Then I felt a kiss on my forehead. That was the last I heard while I slipped into a deep sleep. What an eventful day.

CHAPTER

6

Six days later, I was sitting on the window seat upstairs when I saw five wolves coming through the trees in the woods. I looked close to see if I could figure them out. I knew they were the boys, but I wanted to see if I could make out who was so. I jumped off my seat and ran downstairs and out the back door. All five wolves stopped and looked at me. They started to shift when I yelled, "STOP!" They all looked at me with wide eyes and just stood there.

"I want to figure out if I can guess who you all are."

So I pointed to the first one, and he stepped forward. I could see the smirk on his face. I walked around his body and then got down on my knees to look at his face. He was a sandy-blond color with wicked blue eyes that looked like a storm. I could see white moving around his eyes like the clouds move. I turned my head to the side and squinted my eyes.

I stood up after a couple of minutes and said, "This is Eric, right?"

The wolf looked at me in shock and nodded his head yes. I jumped up and down and did a weird little dance. I picked up his shorts and handed them to him. He put them in his mouth and walked to the trees.

I turned to look at the others, and they were all just sitting there smiling at me. I had an ear-to-ear smile on my face. I pointed to the next wolf. This went on for the next three wolves. They were all brown with odd brown-like-mud eyes. I had a hard time getting them right because they all looked so much alike. But I did get them right, so I was surprised. I stepped up to the last wolf already knowing it was Asher. I started to walk around him, and he stood up. He was pure black so with white paws. As I got to the back of him, I saw that there was a white tip to his tail. I walked back to the front of him, and we were nose to nose. I did not even notice he was this tall. I lifted my head to look at his eyes. They were an awesome green color. It looked like the moss growing on the side of a tree. He bowed his head and nudged me with his nose. I raised my hand and scratched behind his hear. I noticed that part of his ear was missing and ran my hand over it. He let out a little whimper. I stepped back and told him to shift and handed him his shorts. He went behind a tree and, seconds later, came out with a naked chest.

I could not take my eyes off him. I stared at his neck and saw a vein there that was throbbing. I moved down to his pecks, and they were nice and round and strong looking. Next my eyes moved down to his six-pack, and I knew I was drooling now because I just wanted to lick him. Slowly my eyes moved down to his V that was sticking out of the top of his shorts. I licked my bottom lip and heard a growl. I snapped my eyes up to his and saw that his eye was changing colors from blue to black. The guys let out small laughs watching us. I noticed that there was blood coming off the side of this face. I stepped up to him and slowly put my hand on his cheek so he would turn his head. I pushed back his hair to look at his ear. There was a little chunk missing out of it. I grabbed his hand and started to pull him into the house and made him sit on a chair in the kitchen. I walked over the cabinet and grabbed the first aid kit. I walked back over and sat on the table with my legs on each side of him.

I pushed his hair back to get a better look at his ear as I felt his hands rest on my thighs. I grabbed some wipes to clean up his ear to get the blood and mud out of it.

"You want to tell me what happened?"

He hissed in pain as I rubbed his ear, so I started to blow on his ear. His hands tightened on my thighs. He took a breath in and let it out shaky. I hoped he was okay.

"There were rouges on our land, and I had to fight them. One got a hold on my ear and bit down on it. It looks worse than it is."

I placed the wipe on the table beside me and grabbed some cream to rub on his ear. I lightly rubbed it on while I hummed a little song. I felt Asher's hands slowly start to get higher on my thigh.

Now is not the time for this. I must make sure he is okay.

After I was done with the cream, I put a Band-Aid on his ear, and he hissed in pain again. I leaned forward and kissed his ear hoping that would help him feel a little bit better, or maybe take his mind off his ear. Asher grabbed my thighs as he stood, taking me with him. I wrapped my arms around his neck afraid he will drop me.

"Are the rouges gone now?" I asked as he walked up the stairs carrying me.

"Yes, little one, they are gone now. However, we have no idea what they were looking for. It did not make any sense to us as to what brought them here."

I tucked my head into his neck knowing what they want—me. Since I left home, I had been running from my parents. I was sure they were their gang of idiots looking for me. I was going to have to run again and leave Asher behind. I could not let him get hurt again because of me. I tucked my head into his shoulder and sniffed his scent.

I am going to miss him so much. One last night with him, and I will run away before he wakes up. I hope he does not go looking for me. I need him safe, and hopefully next time we meet, he will have his mate.

Asher walked into the bedroom and set me on the bed. He told me he needed to shower and then walked away. I got up and walked over to his nightstand and pulled out a paper and pen. I needed to leave him a note.

Dear Asher,

> You have been my rock for these last couple of months. Thank you for taking me in and watching over me. I have never met anyone like you. You have a heart of gold, and I hope you find your mate soon. I must leave because of those rouges. They are looking for me. My parents will never let me be. I wish I could stay with you, but I cannot see you hurt again. Your ear is my fault. I will never forgive myself for you getting hurt because of me. Do not try to find me. I do not

even know where I am going, but I have saved a lot of money from working with you. Thank you once again. I love you, Asher. I have never felt this way about anyone. Live your life and forget all about me. I will hold you in my heart forever.

Always yours, with love,
Willow

I folded the letter up and put his name on the front of it. I would leave it on the kitchen table when I left in the morning. Asher came out of the bathroom in his boxers and climbed into bed patting the space next to him. I climbed in and lay up against him, enjoying his heat. I knew I was going to be cold after tonight. I had my bag all ready to go because I never unpacked my emergency bag. I had been putting my spare money in there so I would not have to look for anything. It was downstairs in the kitchen under the sink.

I hope I can leave this man. I wish he were my mate.

Asher pulled me closer to him and smelled my hair. He kissed me on the forehead.

"Good night, Willow."

"Good night, Asher."

I lay there listening to his breathing getting shallower. His heartbeat slowed down, and I knew he was asleep. I looked at his face one more time. I leaned over and kissed his lips.

"I love you, Asher. I hope you never forget me no matter what my letter says."

I got up and walked to the bathroom. I did my business and got dressed. I opened the door with the light still on just so I could look at Asher one more time. I gave a deep sigh and walked to the nightstand on my side. I picked up my letter and walked out of the room. I went downstairs and walked to the kitchen. I picked up my backpack and then walked to the table and placed the note on it. I turned around and looked at the house one more time before opening the door and walking out for the last time.

CHAPTER

I walked to the woods and placed my backpack down and thought of a wolf. I wanted to be a big wolf so I could carry my backpack in my mouth. I thought of Asher and began to shift. When I opened my eyes, I laughed in my head. I knew that would not work. I was still little. I picked up my backpack in my teeth and started to run.

I did not know how long I ran for, but the sun was starting to come up. I stopped at the edge of the woods and began to shift back into my human form. Once I was human again, I got dressed and threw my backpack onto my shoulder. I had no idea what town I was in. I did not even know what state I was in. I walked into the little town trying to find somewhere I could lie down and not be seen.

I found an alley and headed down it. There were several boxes in there, so I moved them around and made a little fort. I placed my bag under my head and fell asleep as soon as my eyes closed.

I did not know how long I had slept, but I woke up to a little boy poking me a stick.

"Hey, lady, is you awake? Heck, are you alive?"

I growled a little and opened one eye. I could see this little guy standing there. He had black hair that covered his ears and cute little dimples. His clothes looked brand new. I smiled at the little guy and asked his name.

"I'm Jake!"

"Hello, Jake. I am Willow."

"Willow, why are you sleeping out here in your human form?"

I knew my mouth was hung open and my eyes were wide. *Does he know me? Where the heck am I?*

"I just got into town from running all night, and I am tired. I just fell asleep and didn't think about it."

Jake looked at me for a minute or two before he nodded his little head.

"If you change into your wolf, I will carry your bag and take you to the pack house. They will help you. They do not like wolves being homeless."

I smiled at this little guy and told him to turn around. He did, and I dropped my clothes and thought of a wolf. If this little guy thought I was a wolf, then I would be a wolf. My bones popped and snapped. I felt the fur grow, and then I was lying on the ground catching my breath. I let a little yap, and Jake turned around.

"You are so cute and little. I'm going to be a big wolf. I just know it."

I could not help but smile in my head. Jake told me to follow him. We walked out of the alley and into the town. I was afraid of others seeing me, but Jake seemed to be okay with it.

We got to a big house, and I was guessing that was the pack house. I started to shake, afraid of what would be said. But Jake turned to the left and went to a smaller house about ten feet away from the big house. We stopped on the porch, and he rang the doorbell. An older man opened the door and looked down at Jake.

"Hey, little man, what have you found?" he asked, looking at me.

Jake looked at me and smiled. "This is my friend Willow. I found her in town in an alley sleeping in her human form. Is the alpha here?"

The older man's eyes hazed over, and I knew he was talking to someone. He then looked at Jake and told him he would be right out. I sat on my furry butt looking at everything going on. I smelled oranges and the woods as someone walked to the door. My head slowly rose as I took this man in. His thighs were huge. His waist was narrow. His chest could be seen, and he had an eight-pack. I had never seen one of those. His arms looked like he could pick up a car or truck. Finally, I got to his face. He had a great-looking brown beard. His nose looked like it had been broken and sat to the side just a little bit. I made it to his eyes, and they were a mix between brown and green—hazel. His hair was long and pulled into a ponytail at his neck. You could see tattoos on his arms and neck, but I could not make out what they all were.

He looked down at me and tilted his head to the side and sniffed the air. He knew I was not a wolf but could not figure out what I was by the looks of it.

"Jake, where did you find this wolf?" he said in a deep, gruff voice.

It sent goose bumps all over my furry body. Jake looked at me, then back to the alpha. He looked like he was confused as to what was going on.

"I found her in an alley in town, sleeping. I brought her here because I know we do not let wolves go homeless in this town. She can do work around here and have a roof over her head, so she doesn't have to sleep outside."

The alpha looked at me again.

"Jake, it is just a wolf. They hunt and live outside, not here with us."

Jake looked at me and smiled. He turned to the alpha and asked if they could go to his backyard. The alpha let out a sigh and nodded his head yes. So I, Jake, the older man, and the alpha went into the backyard. Jake looked at me and pulled out my clothes that I had on earlier.

"Where did you get that bag, Jake?" asked the older man.

"It is her bag. She was using it like a pillow while she slept."

Both the men looked at me, then at Jake. They shook their heads like they did not believe us. I felt horrible for putting Jake through this, but he seemed to be having fun. His smile just kept getting bigger and bigger.

"Shift now!" the alpha yelled at me.

I jumped high in the sky and landed with a thud. I put my paws over my eyes, whimpering. Jake ran to me and started to pet me, telling me it would be okay and that the alpha would not hurt me. Slowly I opened my eyes and looked up at him. His eyes were sad just for a minute before they turned hard again. I looked at Jake, and he stood up and turned around. I looked at the older man, and he also turned around. I looked at the alpha, and he stood there with his arms crossed on his chest, just looking at me.

Okay, looks like he will see me naked.

I started to think of my human form, and my body started to snap and pop. As soon as I knew I was human, I was grabbing my clothes. I heard someone take in a sharp breath.

"Lift your head and look at me, shape-shifter."

I whimpered and started to lift my head. First, I looked at Jake, and he was smiling from ear to ear. I think Jake was happy to prove his alpha wrong. Next, I looked at the older man, and he was cracking up with tears running down his face.

"Oh my gosh, Jake just proved you wrong. Way to go, little guy," the older man said.

I smiled at that. Then I looked at the alpha. A voice started to jump around in my mind as our eyes connected.

The last thing I heard before I passed out was the alpha yelling, "MATE!"

CHAPTER

My eyes slowly opened and then slammed back shut from the brightness.

My word, it is bright today.

I opened my eyes again and rubbed them, hoping that would help. I looked in front of me and saw a white ceiling. I started to move my eyes around and saw white walls, a brown door, and black chair and couch. I really felt like freaking out because I had no idea where I was. I tried to think back to the last thing I remembered. Let us see.

1. Running from Asher.
2. Getting to a little town.
3. Waking up to little Jake.
4. Turing into a wolf.
5. Following Jake to a house.
6. An older man laughing hard.
7. Mate! Oh, crap.

My heartbeat started to go faster, and my breathing picked up big time.

I need to get out of here before someone finds me here.

I was getting out of bed when I heard the door handle move. My eyes were wide when I thought of someone finding me. Without even thinking hard, I turned myself into a rabbit and jumped under the blankets. I folded my ears down so they were not sticking out. I watched as a lady came walking into the room. She stopped and looked around trying to find me. I heard her chuckle and walk over to the bed.

"Willow, please come out. I am not going to hurt you. My name is Lexi, and I am a nurse here in the pack house. Please come out so we can talk and I can check you out from fainting."

Taking a deep breath, I moved out from the pillow but kept my ears down. She smiled at me as she reached down to pick me up. She cradled me in her arms close to her heart. She ran her hands down my back several times before she scratched behind my ear. My foot started to twitch with each scratch.

Man, that felt good.

"Willow, do you think you can turn back for me so I can listen to your heartbeat? I will even turn around and not look. As much as I love having you as a rabbit, I need to check on you," she said while smiling at me.

I nodded my little head at her, and she set me on the bed. I watched as she turned around toward the door. After a minute or two, I was back in the bed fully dressed again.

"Okay, I'm ready," I said in a quiet voice.

She turned around and smiled at me with big eyes. Slowly she walked up to me like she was afraid to spook me, which I understand. I get spooked easily.

"Hello, Willow, I'm just going to listen to your heart and take your blood pressure. Is that okay with you?"

I nodded my head, and she got to it—first my heartbeat, then my pressure. She smiled after she was done writing it down on a clipboard.

"Honey, you sound great, and everything checks out simply fine. We had to give you fluids as you have not been drinking enough."

"I'm sorry about that. I ran all night and only stopped a couple of times to drink out of a river or creek. But now that I am here, I can start drinking again," I said, smiling up at Lexi.

"You want to tell me where you are from and what made you come here?" she asked me.

My eyes went wide, and I started to worry what they would think if I told them everything.

"I'm just looking for a new place to live and start a life. My parents wouldn't give my papers to get a job, so I have been living as different animals for shelter and food," I said, looking down.

She looked at me with sad eyes before she hazed over. I knew she was talking to someone, just not sure who. She smiled at me when she came back.

"Well, you can stay with me in my house for the time being. We can get you a job around here if you would like. It does not pay a lot, but you do not have to pay for shelter or food."

I smiled up at her and nodded my head fast. Lexi laughed at me and told me to get dressed and she would show me around. Now, the whole time, I had not even thought of my mate. I did not have time for a guy while I tried to get my life together. Lexi picked up my backpack and walked to the door, waiting on me.

We stepped out of the room into a long white hall with several wood doors. We went to the left and walked out double doors to the outside. The sun was high in the sky, giving off some warmth on this cool day. There were tress all over the place to the right of us and several houses to the left of us. We walked for a little while until we came to a small house that was pink.

Wow, pink.

I had never seen a pink house before and chuckled. Lexi looked at me over her shoulder and laughed too.

"I'm guessing you are laughing at my pink house, right?"

"I have never seen a pink house before!"

"It is Jake's favorite color, so we painted it last year. However, I think he did it just to see if I would follow through with doing it. He is a sweet kid."

I smiled big at the thought of Jake.

"Is Jake your kid?" I asked.

"Yes, he is. He is five and full of energy. Hard to keep up with him. I hear he is the one that brought you here. Is that right?"

"Yes, he found me in an alley in town and brought me here. He is an awesome kid," I said, smiling from ear to ear.

She smiled at me, and we walked up to the green door. I could not help but laugh at the door. Lexi rolled her eyes and opened the door. Before I knew it, I was attacked by a happy Jake who ran into my legs screaming my name.

"WILLOW, YOU ARE HERE! YOU ARE ALIVE!"

Both Lexi and I were laughing at Jake.

"Hey, little man. Good to see you again!"

"I'm glad you are okay. And even better, you are staying with us!" Jake said.

This kid might do me in before the week was up. I smiled at him and gave him a big hug. We stepped into the house, and it was small and cozy. My kind of a home. The living room was to the right, and the kitchen to the left. There was a small hallway between the two rooms at the back. There was Jake's room on the right, a guest room on the left, a bathroom next to Jake's room, and then Lexi's room next to mine. We sat down in the living room as Jake went outside to play.

"Willow, I need to tell you a few things so they don't come up in front of Jake."

I nodded my head for her to continue.

"First, Jake's dad is dead. We had a rouge attack last year, and his dad did not make it. Second, the alpha is your mate, but he is already with someone else. They are not mated, but he plans on making her his Luna. He is twenty-eight and got tired of waiting for you. I'm sorry to be the one to tell you that."

She hung her head down toward the ground. I wrapped my arms around her and pulled her to me.

"It is not your fault that he did not wait for me. If that is the way he wants it, then that is okay with me. I will stay for a week and heal fully before I move on. I do not want to cause any problems."

"But, Willow, you are the true Luna. Everyone will know when they see you or talk to you."

"It is okay. Just let me work where he is not at, and after a week, I will move on. Sometimes mates are not meant to be. After the life I have had, why would my mate be any different? May I take a shower?"

She nodded her head yes with sad eyes. I knew she wanted to ask me what I meant. But I did not want to tell anyone here about my past. I was only here for a week, and then I would go back to Asher. I prayed he would take me back and not be upset with me. I missed him so much. Maybe he would be my mate now.

I got into the hot shower letting the water run down my body, washing the dirt away.

This is heaven.

I grabbed the shampoo and worked it up and then rinsed it out. Next, I grabbed the bodywash and was working it around my body when I hit Asher's bite. I let out a moan. How could I forget about that?

I tried to think. *I think I have two weeks before the heat starts again. By then, I will be back with Asher.*

I touched the bite again, and goose bumps formed on my body. I could feel his hands on my body and his hot breath on my ear.

Come back to me. I need you, Asher whispered in my ear.

I jumped thinking it was really him and looked around. I hung my head down when I did not find him. I should have just told him the truth instead of running. I washed my body and rinsed before drying and getting dressed.

I walked back into the living room to see Lexi looking at me with worried eyes.

"Hey, what is wrong?"

"The alpha has called a pack dinner. Everyone must go. So you have to go with us."

I knew my eyes were as big as basketballs by the time she was done talking. I did not want to go. I could not go. I did not want to see anyone while here. Just stay low. So much for that idea.

"Okay, let's do this."

CHAPTER

We walked into the pack house, and I was amazed at how big it was. I knew there was a lot of people here, but I had no idea it was this many. I could feel the sweat of my hands. I could feel my face start to heat up as we got closer to the door. Lexi took my hand and gave it a squeeze. With my head held up high, I walked into the dining hall. I looked around the room; everyone seemed to be already in their seats. All eyes looked at me. I stopped walking and did not even know it until Lexi pulled my hand. I looked at her and started to walk with her to the seats. Jake was already sitting there waving at me. I let out a breath I did not know I was holding and walked up to Jake.

"Hi, Willow! I have missed you today" came from Jake.

I smiled at him and sat next to him. I looked around the room and took it all in. Everyone was sitting at big wood tables with little wood stools to sit on, almost looked like tree trunks. Everyone had white plates in front of them with plastic forks. It looked like it was the throwaway stuff, but it was heavy. So that meant that it was not the throwaway stuff. There were big wildflowers in the middle of each table. Everyone was talking again and waiting for the alpha to walk in so they could eat.

It got quiet, and everyone bowed their heads. Jake pulled my hand so I would bow my head also. I looked up just with my eyes and saw only a figure, so I put my eyes down.

"I would like everyone to welcome the alpha of Dark Moon pack. Plus, I also want to announce my new Luna, Shelley. Now, everyone, have a nice meal," came the big voice of the alpha.

Everyone started to look up, and plates were set onto the other plates sitting on the table. A steak and baked potatoes were on the new plate. My mouth started to water. I knew I was hungry but not this bad. I took my first bite and let out a little moan. This was mouthwatering. I felt eyes on me but just did not care to look around and see who it was. There were small talk going around. I did not talk much, just a head nod every now and them.

Jake nudged me in my side, and I looked up at him. He moved his eyes to the left for me to look that way. I moved my eyes slowly in the area he was looking at and saw that the alpha was looking at me. I smiled at him and went back to my food.

If he wants another woman, that is fine. I can always go back to Asher, if he will take me back.

Lexi placed her fork down, and I felt her eyes on my face. So I looked up to see what was going on. Her eyes were wide, and she was looking up and over me. I placed down my fork and looked up to see what was going on. My eyes bugged out of my head when I saw Asher standing there.

I jumped out of my chair and into his arms. His big arms wrapped around my back as he pulled me closer to him. I smelled him and just enjoyed the heat from his body. Asher buried his face into my neck, and I felt him smell me. I have missed this man more than I thought. I never wanted to let go of him.

"Where have you been? Why are you here? What happened? Why did you leave me?" Asher whispered in my ear.

I felt so bad for leaving him. For putting him through all of this. I never wanted to let go again.

He is mine. I do not care about having a mate or him having one. He is mine.

"The rouges are after me. I felt horrible that you got hurt. I never want to see you hurt because of me, so I ran. I ran all night and woke up here the next afternoon and was brought here. I did not want to leave you. It broke my heart to leave you. I never want to leave you again. I want to go back home with you, please," I cried into his neck.

He held me tighter and nodded his head yes. I was so overcome with happiness that I did not notice the alpha walking up to us. My body was yanked out of Asher's arms and moved behind a back.

Wow, this back is huge.

I looked over to side to see Asher standing there with a glare on his face.

"You want to explain why you just ripped her out of my arms?" Asher asked.

I could hear the ticked off in his voice.

"I don't have to explain myself to you, but you don't come into my pack just picking up my people and hugging them. I don't care who you are," the alpha said, ticked off.

I saw his mate walking over to us. She looked like the pack slut. She placed her hand on his arm and whispered to him to calm down. I laughed in my head at that one. The alpha looked back at me over his shoulder and breathed out a breath. I did not know what his problem was. He picked someone else, so I could pick someone else. I just needed to know his name so I could reject him. He looked back at Asher and asked him to come back to the table to finish the meal. Asher looked at me and winked. He walked away, so I sat back down and started eating.

Everyone got back to what they were doing, or so I thought. Everyone got quiet again, all eyes moving the same way. I looked up to see what was going on, and Asher was walking through the dining hall carrying his plate. What is he doing? He came to stand behind me and set his plate next to mine. He then put his arms under my arms and picked me up from my chair. He then sat down in my chair and placed me on his lap. I turned bright red with where I was sitting and looked at Lexi. She looked like she was about to blow up with laughter. Next we hear was a loud, mean growl. I looked up at the alpha, and his eyes were turning black.

Great, now he is ticked even more.

Asher leaned forward to my ear and asked me what his deal is.

"You are not going to believe if I tell you."

"How bad can it be, Willow? Just tell me," Asher begged me.

I closed my eyes and took a deep breath. "He is my mate. But he has chosen someone else. So I need his name so I can reject him."

Asher took a deep breath and let it out slowly. He looked up at the alpha, then back at me. He tightened his hold on me. I did not know what was going on, but I knew that Asher nor the alpha were happy right now. I leaned into Asher, afraid that this alpha would grab me again. He got up and started to walk toward us.

Asher pulled me closer to him and whispered in my ear, "He can't have you. I will not let him have you."

I relaxed a little in his arms.

"Oh, and his name is David Smith."

I smiled up at Asher, and he winked at me.

"Can we all talk in the hall where all these eyes are not on us?" the alpha asked.

I looked at Asher, and he nodded his head. We got up and walked out.

"Asher, I don't know what is going on, but you keep touching her, and I don't like it. Get your hands off her!" the alpha yelled.

Asher smiled at me, then turned to the alpha. "Let me ask you a question or two. Do you feel a strong pull to her or a little one? Do you plan on getting rid of Shelley for Willow? Will you be a good mate to her?"

"How did you know? Did she tell you?" he asked, pointing to me.

I smiled up at Asher. Asher winked at me as he turned to the alpha, which earned a growl from him.

"Yes, she told me, but I can also see it because you keep coming over here and talking to me about touching her. You have always been easy to read, David."

"I plan on keeping Shelley and not letting her go ever. I plan on keeping Willow too because she is the only one that can have my children. I will have both, and you need to keep your hands off her."

I opened my mouth to reject him, but Asher said not to yet. He had one thing to say.

"You don't feel a strong pull to her because I have already bit her. She has my mark on her already. She has gone through heat once already because of it. She is mine now, and you hold no claim on her. She will be leaving with me and going back to my pack. There will be no war. There will be no 'you are looking for her.' You will let her go and be with just Shelley. Willow is now mine."

I smiled big because I loved the feel of Asher saying I was his. I looked up at Asher, and he told me, "Now." So I looked at the alpha.

"I, Willow Storm, reject you, Alpha David Smith, as my mate. I no longer hold any ties to you. You are free to love another." I felt a pain in my heart as I said this.

The alpha grabbed his heart and let out a sorrow howl. Asher grabbed my hand and walked to the door. I looked back and saw the alpha on his knees with his head in his hands. We stepped outside; and Asher walked over to a pickup truck, opened the door, and helped me in.

Guess I am going back with Asher now.

CHAPTER

We got to the edge of David's territory and heard a horrible howl. Asher stepped on the gas to get us across a line I could not see. He let out a breath he was holding and slowed down the truck. I was starting to sweat because I did not think we were far enough from David. Asher looked at me from the corner of his eyes. He took a deep breath and let it out. I just sat waiting for the questions to start. Once again, he took a deep breath, and I chuckled a little.

"Asher, just ask me already. I can't read your mind, but I don't mind talking about it," I finally said to him.

"I don't have too many questions, but the one that is the biggest is why are the rouges looking for you?"

I took a deep breath and got ready to tell him everything. "Okay, so here we go."

"I was four years old when my dad hit me for the first time. I spilled my milk in the living room on the carpet. He slapped me across my little face and sent me flying into the wall. I cried and cried, and he just walked away. The next time he hit me was when I was ten. I messed up the laundry by putting a red sock in with his white clothes. Everything turned pink. I was pulled up by my hair and thrown down the stairs. I landed on the concrete floor and hit my head a couple of times on the stairs on the way down. My eyes were blurry, and my head was pounding. I lifted my head to see if I could see anything.

"I saw my mom sitting on a couch down there, so I crawled over to her. As I got closer to her, she lifted her foot up and kicked me in the chest. I fell over again, gasping for breath. My mom got up and pulled me up by my hair and dragged me over to a table. She picked me up and placed me on the table. I was screaming and crying while they tied me down to the table. My dad got a belt and started to hit my legs and tummy. I was screaming, and they did not care. My mom then took a hot branding iron and started to put it under my left breast.

"After what felt like hours, they walked away and left me there bleeding and crying. I passed out after a while and woke up when it was dark outside. My mom was untying me. I was taken upstairs and washed and then put into bed. This went on for six years. Sometimes on my front. Sometimes on my back. I had scars from it all and still have the branding under my breast. I ran from them one night. My body started to snap and pop in my room. It hurt so bad that I ran outside into the woods so they would not hear me scream.

"I changed into a rabbit and just lay in the grass, shaking. At that point in time, I knew these people were not my real parents. I learned that they were trying to keep me down so I would not change. I went back into my human form and changed. I went into my room and packed my backpack and ran. I was running for two months when they found me. They tied me up and brought me back to their house. It was rouges that found me. They told me that my mommy and daddy were looking for me and that they would get a lot of money for bringing me back. I fought them every step of the way because I did not want to go back. I do not want to be there anymore, nor do I want to be beaten anymore.

"When we got back to the house, I was pulled into the basement and, once again, tied down to the table. I was hit, punched, cut, and whipped with a belt. I had cuts all over me and was bleeding everywhere. After two hours, they went back upstairs, and I closed my eyes. I thought about my skin before I got hit. I thought of how it looked before all of this started. After an hour, my body was healed. I was no longer bleeding. I no longer had cuts, and I no longer was tired and worn out. I fought and pulled until one of my hands was free. I pulled the other ropes off me and made my way to the stairs. I got up to the kitchen and looked around. I did not know where my backpack was, and I was afraid I lost all the money I had.

"I heard walking coming toward me, so I thought of a mouse and changed into it. It was not until then that I noticed that I was naked. I ran along the wall trying to find a hole to get out of. A guy stepped into the room and saw me and started to scream and jump around. I found that funny as all get out. I ran over to the door, and he opened it hoping I would run out. And that I did. I ran as fast as my little feet could go. I got over by the trucks and saw my backpack sitting by a wheel of the black truck. I changed again into a dog and picked it up in my teeth and ran. I got into the woods and took off to the left. I had already been to the right.

"I found a river and jumped over it. I walked a little way away from the river and then turned around and walked the same way I came. I jumped into the river and changed yet again, this time to a turtle that could swim. I hooked my bag around my neck and shell and started to float down the river. I floated all night, then all day, then all night, and then all day again. I waited until the sun went down before I changed back into a human and walked out of the river. I pulled my bag with me and started to set up a fire. I was cold, and all my clothes were wet. Once I got the fire going, I pulled my clothes out of my bag and hung them up around the fire. I was so cold that I changed again into a wolf and got close to the fire. I was hoping the fire would keep my body warm as a wolf.

"I fell asleep, and when I woke up again, the sun was up. I looked around for anything, but all I saw was woods. So I got dressed and packed up my bag and started to walk following the river, hoping it would lead me to a town. I walked for an hour before I came to the cabin in the woods. I looked all around, and there was no one around. The place looked like no one had been there in years. I walked in and took it over as my own. I lived there for six months before you found out about me. Then the rouges came for me again, and I ran again. I do not know why they want me so much. I do not know what I ever done to them. I don't know why they will not give up."

I lowered my head as all the memories played through my head. I felt a warm hand on mine and looked up to see Asher with sad eyes but also what looked like love in them.

Asher started to open his mouth to say something when we heard a war-cry howl. We looked at each other with wide eyes. Asher started to go faster until I screamed, "ASHER! LOOK OUT!"

He looked to the front of him, and there was a wall of wolves across the road. He slammed on the break, and we flew forward in our seats. I saw Asher's eyes go hazed, and I let out a breath. He was calling for backup. He grabbed my hand.

"I will fight to my last breath for you, Willow. You are my mate now. I am not ever letting you go. I love you." Asher let go of my hand and stepped out of the truck. He looked back at me and said, "Stay in the truck. Stay safe." Then he walked in front of the truck.

CHAPTER

I sat in the truck watching what was going on in front of it. Asher was standing with his hands on his hips, and the wolves were just standing there. I rolled my window down just a little bit so I could hear what was going on.

"SHIFT!" That came from Asher. He sounded so mad.

I looked at the wolves and saw one of them start to shift. I saw a wolf come out of the woods with shorts in his mouth. I looked up and saw the beta of David.

Oh no, this is not going to be good.

"What are you doing here?" Asher said.

"We have come for Willow. Come to find out she is our Luna, and she is going back with us," the beta said.

"You do know that she rejected him, right?"

"Alpha David said that it was a mistake, and he wants to chat with her."

"David told her that he was going to keep Shelley as the Luna and Willow as the one to carry his babies and then show that they are from Shelley. He has a whole plan to fool you guys." Asher said, getting mad just thinking about it.

"Alpha said you would say something along those lines to mislead us. We are here to get our Luna and take her back. There is nothing you can do, so hand her over. No fighting," David said with his head held high.

Asher just stood there for a minute, just thinking of what to do or say. He looked like he was wasting time. Maybe he was waiting for his backup. I heard a voice out my window right after I thought that.

"Willow, don't scream. It is me, Eric. We are here to help. There are twenty of us here. I need you to stay calm. Get down on the floorboard. Maybe change shapes or something down there so it is hard to see you. Please."

I slowly slipped onto the floorboard and became a spider. I lay on the floorboard just waiting for what would happen. I heard all the voices even as a spider.

"I don't understand why he needs Shelley and Willow. He doesn't need both," Asher said.

"It is not up to you to say what the alpha needs or doesn't need. Now hand her over."

"My beta no longer has a mate as Shelley was it. She rejected him and told him that she loves David. She chooses him over my beta. He accepted the rejection, and he is moving on. Willow rejected David because he has Shelley and told Willow that. He does not want her for anything but breeding. Willow wants to be my mate, and I want her. You need to back off and get off my land," Asher said.

Oh crap, they are on Asher's land. That will not go well. They did not ask him to come on to the land.

I climbed up onto the dashboard so I could see what was going on. I saw that the beta had stepped closer to Asher. I saw that the other wolves were trying to get closer to the truck without Asher noticing. But I know Asher. He knew what they were doing. The beta took another step forward, getting almost to Asher. Eric was back at my window.

"Willow, I am going to open your door. I am going to do it quietly. I need you to not freak out and to stay in the truck. We want it to look like you have left the truck. I have no clue if you can hear me or understand me." Eric let out a breath and opened the door. He backed up away from the truck toward the back.

I turned back to Asher to see what was going on up there.

Asher raised his hands up in the air. I noticed he only had four fingers in the air.

I am so confused right now.

"I will let you check my truck for her. But she will not be there. I dropped her off a little way back when we saw the wolves in the road. Her door is opened from her jumping out. I do not know where she is. I don't know where she is going." Asher's finger dropped to a three.

The beta's eyes went hazy. I noticed the wolves nodded their heads yes. The beta stepped to the truck and placed his head into it. I slid down into the vent. He moved stuff around looking everywhere for me.

He smelled my bag and held it up. "Why do you have this if you don't have her? It smells like it is hers."

Asher dropped another finger to two and turned to the beta. "Willow lived with me for several months. I carry that bag with me everywhere in case I find her. It has clothes in it that she would wear. I always have the hope that I could find her again and she would stay with me instead of running."

The beta let out a deep breath and backed away from the truck and went back to the other wolves. "I'm sorry for causing troubles with you, Alpha Asher. I mean no disrespect at all. I hope this does not cause a problem with you and me. I'm just following my alpha's orders." The beta bowed his head and then looked up. "All right, wolves, there is nothing here for us. Let us go back home and tell our alpha what we have found."

The beta turned into a wolf and howled. Everyone started to follow him off the lands. Asher put his hands down and turned to look at the truck.

Eric and the boys stepped out from the trees and from around the back of the truck. Asher stepped up to the truck and called my name. I came out of the vent and looked at him. He chuckled at me and held his hand out for me to climb onto his hand. I climbed onto his hand, and he pulled me closer to him. He opened his pocket for me to go into there. So I made my way in there and changed myself again. This time, I was a sugar glider. I poked my head out and looked up at Asher. He chuckled again at me and pet my little head. He looked at all his guys and told them to meet back at the house after they ran the area and made sure they all left.

Asher got back into the truck. "Willow, I need you to stay like you are until we get home. I do not want anyone to see you just yet.

They will tell the others, and then it will get back to David that I still have you with me. I'm sorry you have to stay like this for now."

He started the truck and started to drive to the house. I climbed out of his pocket and onto his shoulder. I rubbed my furry head on his cheek and just loved on him. He laughed at me and smiled. I went over to his ear and licked it.

Asher jumped, and the truck jerked. "Willow, no. You cannot do stuff like that to me. I might crash the truck and hurt us both."

He started to focus on driving again, then I climbed down into his lap. I started to run my little paws over his manhood. He jumped again and looked down at me. I smiled up at him, and he shook his head.

"Behave, Willow."

I climbed back into his pocket and pouted. I wanted him. I wanted to mess with him some more. So I felt around for his nipple under his shirt. When I found it, I bit it a little bit with my small mouth. He groaned and reached for me and pulled me out of his pocket. He looked at me and told me I was a bad girl for messing with him in animal form. I wanted him, and I wanted him now. His eyes went hazy while he was talking with me. A small smile made its way onto his face. His eyes came back as he looked at me with an evil look.

Oh no, I am in trouble.

He stepped out of the truck. I did not even notice that we stopped. He walked over to the woods and looked around.

"The other wolves are gone now. They are already in the next town over. You want to play? Then turn into a wolf. That is the only way that I will play as an animal," Asher told me.

I smiled at him and started to wiggle in his hands, trying to get free. He set me down on the ground, and I looked up at him, tapping my little foot.

"Oh! You want me to turn first?"

I nodded my head, and he took off to behind a tree.

A minute later, his big black wolf walked out, his blue eyes looking right at me. I have missed those eyes. I started to snap and pop. I wanted to be tied to him. So when he looked at me, his eyes were wide, and his mouth opened. I was standing there as a pure-white wolf but with black-tipped ears and paws. I even had a black-tipped tail. I walked up to him and noticed that I only came to his shoulders.

I hope he does not hurt me by accident.

I started to rub myself on him, trying to snap him out of it. He looked down at me and had a wolf grin on his face. He went to nip at my tail, but I jumped away from him in time. I yapped at him and jumped around, showing I wanted to play.

Asher nudged my hind leg, and I took off running. I could hear his feet pounding into the ground. I started to sniff around thinking I could find the cabin in the woods. I found the river and ran across it. I heard Asher run into it not too far behind me.

I must hurry. He is getting too close to me.

I took off to the right because I knew his house was that way. I finally got into a clearing and saw his house coming closer. I felt Asher right behind me. He jumped on top of me and knocked my feet out from under me. I fell onto my tummy and whimpered. That hurt so bad. He lay down to where he was, still standing up and covering me up at the same time. I heard him let out a growl and looked in front of us to see what was going on.

In front of us, stood an older man. Someone I had never seen before.

"Alpha Asher, please change back to your human form so we can chat. Your little wolf can stay in her form if that makes her feel better, but we need to talk." The man then threw shorts at Asher.

He pulled me with him behind a tree. He changed into his human form and pulled the shorts on. He then picked me up.

"I need you to stay as a wolf. I will always keep you with me, sitting on my lap. Do not play around. This is an elder whom we will show respect to. Please behave, Willow."

I nodded my head while he said, "That is my girl." I yapped at him, and he walked out from behind the tree.

"Elder, would you please follow us into the house, and we will chat in there."

The elder nodded his head and followed Asher into the house. This was going to be a long night.

CHAPTER

12

We sat in the living room, the elder in one chair and Asher in another one with me on his lap. He was petting my head, trying to keep me calm as he felt my little body shake. Asher offered him water, but he did not want anything.

"First and foremost, I am here not to take anyone away from the other. I am not here to break up anyone. What I am here for is to get your side of what has happened and then figure it all out. I will do everything in my power to follow everyone's wishes. Sometimes that is hard to do. But don't think I am here just to pull people apart," the elder said.

I felt my body relax a little. Asher let out a deep breath.

"Elder, what are you here for?" asked Asher after a minute or two.

"We have had several reports about a little shape-shifter named Willow, which, I am guessing, is the little one on your lap. Now, do not worry, little one. I am not here to hurt you or take you away. I am here to hear your side of the story and see what I can do. You see, Asher and I are longtime friends. I don't want to break his heart nor take his life away from him."

I nodded my head at him.

"For the first part of this, you can stay as the wolf you are now. But close to the end, you are going to have to change and talk to me. Okay, let us start. The first report I have is that your mom and dad are looking for you. They have said that you ran away and stole over $20,000 on your way out the door. Now, I do not believe that one at all. Your parents have never had that kind of money. Plus, they are evil people. I have heard some talk about how they abused you, and that is why you ran away. I heard that they used a branding iron on you and that is was three *S*s. Before you ask, we caught two rouges going through our land, and they told us all of that to save their lives, which didn't work by the way." He then winked at me. "Next, we have Alpha David. He has said that you, Asher, broke in and stole his mate from his home and took her away. He said that you beat up a lot of his men and that you told David, if he came after you, you would kill him too and take his land. This one, I tried to keep my laugh in, but it did not work too well. David got mad that I laughed at him." The elder took a breath and looked at us. "Now, we are going to start with Asher about David, and maybe by the time he is done, you will want to change and talk with me." He winked at me which earned him a growl from Asher. The elder just died laughing with tears running down his cheeks. "You, my dear friend, are too easy."

Asher huffed and rolled his eyes. He took a deep breath and looked to the elder. "David called me three days ago and asked me to come to a dinner party that he was having. He said that he was announcing his Luna and wanted me there for it. I thought that was weird since we are not close. I told him that I would be there just for dinner, no longer. I showed up, and right away, I smelled Willow. I figured that was why he wanted me there. He could smell me on Willow. I went in, and they took me to his office for a drink before dinner. I met Shelley who is to be his Luna. I could tell she is the pack slut and could not understand why he picked her. When I smelled her closer, I smelt that she was my beta's mate. It was hard to tell with all the scents on her. She rolled her eyes at me when I figured it out. Shelley's eyes went hazy, and then the next thing I knew, someone was knocking on the door asking the alpha for help. The lady winked at Shelley as David walked out of the office. She did not smell like a Luna, and I knew I did not want that as my beta's mate. I mind-linked my beta and told him what was going on. He linked back that he had already rejected her because of her being the pack slut. We walked downstairs, and I could smell Willow even stronger. We walked in and sat down. My eyes looked at everyone and everywhere, looking for Willow. Then David welcomed me and then announced Shelley. Every clapped for me and little claps for Shelley. I heard her huff and him tell her it would be okay. My eyes never stopped moving trying to find Willow. I saw a little guy waving his hands like crazy, and my eyes stopped on him. He smiled at me and then pointed to the person next to him that had their head down. I looked closer and saw it was Willow. My eyes bugged out, and the little guy nodded his head and smiled from ear to ear. I guess he could smell me on her also.

"I stood up and walked away from the table. David tried to get me to sit back down, but I was not having any of it. I walked up to the back of the little guy and looked down at him, giving him a wink. The lady across from Willow was talking and stopped with wide eyes looking at me. That made Willow look up behind her. She saw me and jumped into my arms. I hugged her back just as tight as she was me. I heard a growl at this point and had no idea whom it was from or why. Next thing I knew, David was standing next to me, yelling at me for touching one of his pack members and that 'we do not do that type of thing' and to put her back down. I set her down and turned to him. He was ticked off, and his eyes were changing between him and his wolf. I just rolled my eyes while he dragged me back to the table, telling me that I could not just pick up people and that I was meant to be at the head table with him to show my support for his new Luna. That was when it hit me that Willow was his mate. That just ticked me off that he was pulling this show. So I picked up my plate and walked back to Willow with him yelling at my back. I placed my plate down. Willow looked up at me, and I grabbed her under her arms and picked her up. I sat down in her chair and set her on my lap and started to eat again.

"David was growling and yelling, and Shelley was trying to calm him down. That made me laugh because he was just getting more upset. He asked us to take our talk out to the hall. Willow and I followed him into the hall. He then went on to tell me that Willow was his, that he was going to have Willow and Shelley. Shelley would share his bed and be his Luna. Willow would be a breeder and only good for giving him babies. I was not going to stand there and take it. But Willow, she rejected him right then and there. She asked if we could leave then, and I said yes. So Willow and I got in my truck and drove off. When we got back to our land, we had a run-in with David's beta." Asher went on to explain about that while I got up off his lap and climbed the stairs.

I walked into the bedroom and changed into my human form. I found some shorts and one of Asher's shirts. I walked into the bathroom and washed my face and drank some water. I ran a hand through my hair and then walked back downstairs.

This is it. Time to face the music to my past.

I walked over to Asher and sat down by him. He took his hand and held onto mine. I breathed a deep breath and then went on to tell the elder everything that I told Asher earlier. I did not add anything nor take anything away. The elder had tears in his eyes.

"The only thing that I need to explain to you is that I have been stealing food or begging for food. That is how Asher found me. He brought me here as a puppy. He didn't know I was a shape-shifter."

The elder nodded his head. He took a deep breath and asked me the one question I was afraid he would ask.

"Can I see the mark under your breast? You can hold it up and keep your breast covered. But I need to see the mark, just to make sure I found the right person."

I sucked in a deep breath as Asher pulled me to him growling.

"Asher, you will be there the whole time. I would never do anything without you there. You can even put her on your lap."

Asher looked at me, and I nodded my head. The elder let out a breath. Asher picked me up and put me on his lap. He wrapped his big arms around me and pulled me close to him. I looked down and pulled my shirt up a little bit. I made sure that my breast was not hanging out. I pulled my breast up with the shirt to show the underpart. The elder put on a pair of glasses and got on his knees. He came closer to me, and I turned my head into Asher's neck and closed my eyes. I could feel the tears coming out. Asher whispered in my ear sweet nothings. The elder told me I could open my eyes now. I looked up, and he was back in his seat, glasses back in his pocket with tears in his eyes.

"No one should ever be treated that way. Thank you for letting me see it. Now I know you are the one they are looking for. I have an idea, but I'm not sure you guys will like it at all."

Asher and I looked at each other, then back at the elder.

"What is your idea?" I asked in a small voice.

"I have medicine with me that will numb that area. We cut it off, and I give it to your parents, saying that you were found and killed for stealing from them. Then, Asher, you bite her and make her your mate. Then her smell will change, and no one will know who she is. But you cannot bite her until the skin is off. Otherwise, the skin will give off her new scent. David will not know that she has changed her smell. You can shape-shift, so if David is ever around, you can change the way you look. He will never know the difference because he is stupid."

I lost my breath. Cut my skin? Could I live through that kind of pain? Could Asher handle that kind of pain?

"Willow, when I cut your skin, the pain will be great for David. He will feel it all. The medicine that I give you will slow down your heart to where David will think that you died from it. He will lose his mating connection with you. He will believe you died. While you are coming out of it, that is when Asher will mark you. David will not feel it, and you will come back as Asher's mate. David will lose you forever, and your parents will believe you are dead. What do you guys think?"

I took a deep breath and slowly let it out. I looked up at Asher.

"I'm up for it if you can handle the pain," I said to Asher.

Asher looked at me and came forward to kiss my forehead.

"Let's do this," Asher said.

CHAPTER

I climbed up on to the steel table getting ready to be strapped down. I took a deep breath and looked up at Asher. I gave him a weak smile and once again breathed in.

"Willow, just keep breathing and keep your eyes on me for the first little bit. Once the medicine kicks in, you will be out cold. In other words, you will be asleep," the elder said to me.

I nodded my head and closed my eyes, slowing my heart rate down.

I felt hands on my wrist and looked up to see who it was. Asher had a hold of me, pulling my wrist into the strap. After he buckled my right wrist, he moved on to my left one. Next, he moved to my ankles, locking each one of them down. Asher leaned down and kissed my forehead and moved to my ear to whisper to me.

"I love you and will see you when you wake up."

Then he plunged the needle into my neck. My eyes got heavy fast, and I felt dizzy. I was still aware of Asher and the elder talking to each other getting me ready. The elder was telling him what he was going to have to do while I was out of it. I opened my eyes and looked up to see Asher standing over me, watching me.

"It is okay, Willow. Just close your eyes and dream of your future," Asher said to me.

I did not know when I was awake or asleep, but I felt like I felt it all. I felt Asher's hands as he removed my shirt from my neck and sliced it open to get to my breast. Then, I felt the knife cut my bra off so they could get to the scar under my breast. I know I drifted off to sleep for a little bit after that, but I jerked up when I felt the edge of the knife going into my skin. I tried to let out a scream, but I felt like I was underwater and that no one could hear me. I felt my skin being cut and pulled away from my body. I wanted them to stop. It hurt way too bad, but they could not hear me while I screamed in my head.

I heard the elder speaking, "Okay, let us put that on ice to keep it fresh for her parents. Then, we can clean her up and get her ready for death."

My heart started to slow down more to where I was having a hard time focusing on anything. I felt my skin getting wiped down. I felt a kiss on my forehead.

I heard phone ringing in the background of my mind.

Who could be calling me right now? Who wants to call me at a time like this? Don't they know that I am dying right now?

"Hello?" That sounded like Asher to me.

I heard a laugh that was deep and made shivers run down my spine.

"Yes, Willow is dead. I am sorry, David, but you sent all those wolves after her. They are the ones that killed her. We did not know if she would live. We brought her back to my pack house. She died there."

It was quiet for a little bit while I tried to keep breathing. It was getting hard as my lungs felt so heavy and waterlogged.

"No, you never loved her. You picked someone else. I will give her a burial here, and you can just move on with your new wife and leave Willow to a peaceful death.

"David, I said no! You stay there and leave Willow in peace. Yeah, same to you. Goodbye."

I heard Asher let out a deep breath and slam the phone down on something.

"You did good, Asher. Do not let him get to you. He now thinks Willow is dead. We need to be taking care of her and not worrying about David," the elder said.

"You are right. I'm sorry, Elder. What do we do now?"

"We clean her up and move her upstairs to your bed. In about one hour, she will wake up, and you will need to mark her before she is fully awake."

I heard Asher let out a big breath and agreed with the elder. I felt water on me while they cleaned me up and then had something put under my breast. I let my mind go to sleep so I could wake up with Asher. The pain I was feeling was great, and I did not know if I would be able to enjoy the marking with the way I was feeling. I was worried about making Asher sick with the medicine I had flowing through me. I felt my body being lifted and pulled into a warm chest. I snuggled up to it, trying to warm myself up. I heard a chuckle and knew it was Asher laughing at me.

"I will see you guys tomorrow morning. Now remember, Asher, mark her before she fully wakes up, or David will feel her."

"Yes, sir. See you tomorrow."

The last thing I remembered was my body being laid down onto a soft bed and sleep fully taking me over.

CHAPTER

I slowly opened my eyes and looked around the dark-lit room. My heartbeat started to pick up, not sure where I was. I felt a hand on my waist and tried to scream, but my throat was dry. I tried to move away from the hand, but it just pulled me in closer.

How am I going to get away from this? I cannot see anything. I cannot smell anything. Where the hell am I?

"Willow, it is okay. Just breathe. It is me, Asher. You are in my room. Take deep breaths," I heard Asher say.

I started to slow my breathing down and closed my eyes to try to focus on what had happened. I moved to the left and felt a pull under my breast. Everything came rushing back to me—the medicine, the removing of my scar, David thinking I was dead, and the marking that had not happened yet. I felt Asher move to the right of me and tried to focus on him. He got up out of bed and headed for a door. About five minutes later, he came back with a glass of water. He kneeled next to me and lifted my head a little for me to drink. The soothing cold water flowed down my throat for sweet relief.

"Willow, I need you to focus. We need to mark you before you wake up too much. We can't have David feel that you are alive," came Asher's sweet voice.

I opened my eyes and looked up to him. He had a look of worry on his face. I raised my hand up to touch his face and ran my hand over his jaw. I took a deep breath and nodded my head for him to start.

Asher slowly lay back down by me and pulled me closer to him. His hand held my face with the right side while his thumb ran circles around my cheek.

"You are so beautiful. I can't wait to have you as my mate forever," came Asher's whisper.

I was so excited to be tied to this man forever. Asher pulled me closer to him and was lying half on top of me. The medicine was still in my system, making me feel like I was underwater.

In my head, I was thinking, *Just mark me so I can go back to sleep.*

I felt Asher's mouth on my neck while he kissed me, trying to find my sweet spot. When I let out a low moan, he looked up at me and smirked.

"I found it. I hope this doesn't hurt, but I will take care of you always."

Asher placed his lips back on my neck in the same place and kissed me again. I let out a small moan as I felt his tongue run over the spot. I felt Asher take a deep breath and then felt his teeth go into my skin. I let out a scream from the burning feeling. It felt like a hot poker iron was shoved into my neck. Asher held me close trying to take the pain away. I felt his teeth come out of my neck and his tongue run over it to close it up. I let out a small moan for the actions of his tongue. Asher lay back down on the bed rubbing my arm.

"I love you, Willow" was the last thing I heard as I fell back into the heavy water.

I woke the next day with the sun shining on my face. I looked around the room and saw that I was in Asher's room, but he was not in here anywhere. Slowly I got out of bed and stood on shaky legs. I walked over to the bathroom and opened the door, stepping inside. I looked in the mirror, and it looked like I had a massive hangover. There were black bags under my eyes; my hair was everywhere. I looked down at my neck and could not believe my eyes. I did not remember getting marked. On the right side of my neck, by my shoulder, was a little black wolf with the name Asher under it. It was the most beautiful thing I had ever seen. I ran my hand over it, and it sent tingles down my spine as a moan slipped from my lips.

I dropped my hand and turned to start the shower. I stepped inside when it was warm enough. I stood there letting the water run down my body, relaxing all my muscles. After a little while, I washed my hair and rinsed it out. I got the bodywash and started to wash my body. My hand froze when I got to my under breast. I did not feel my scar. I did not feel anything. I looked down fast, pulling my breast up. There was nothing but smooth skin. How? Why? What happened to a scar from removing the mark? I was so confused.

I hurried in the shower to finish and stepped out drying myself off. I walked over to the mirror and pulled my breast up to look at it. It was smooth skin, no marks whatsoever. What the heck? I hurried to the closet and pulled on a shirt of Asher's and took off through the house to find him. I looked everywhere before I found him sitting outside on his chair. I ran over to him and stopped in front of him.

"Willow, holy crap, you scared me! Are you okay?"

"Asher, I don't know what is going on. I do not have a scar from the knife removing my scar. Why is the skin smooth?"

Asher looked at me like I was crazy. He stood up and took my hand, leading me back into the house. He took me upstairs to his room. He walked over to the bed and sat down on it, pulling me between his legs where I stood over him. He looked up at me, looking at me with his eyes asking if he could look. I nodded my head and felt his hands being placed on my hips. Slowly he raised his hands and slipped my shirt up. He never took his eyes from my eyes. Once my shirt was up, my breast could be seen. My nipples went hard from the air and from his touch, sending goose bumps all over my body.

His eyes left mine as he looked at my breast. His hand wrapped around my breast as he lifted it up to look under it. Asher's rough hand ran over my smooth skin, feeling the replacement of my scar. His eyes looked up to mine with a questioning look.

"What happened?"

"Asher, I have no idea. I got up and took a shower, and while I was washing, I noticed that there was nothing there. So I got out of the shower and checked it. Why is it so smooth?" I asked with a whisper.

Asher looked down at the smooth skin and ran his hand over it again. Goose bumps broke out all over my body, and a little moan slipped past my lips. Asher's eyes snapped up to me, and I could see his eyes were changing back and forth with black. His wolf was trying to take over.

"Maybe when I marked you, the skin fixed itself. Maybe it healed you," Asher said with some confusion.

I guessed we both would not know what was going on and maybe would never get the answers. Asher pulled me closer to him by his hands on my hips. I slid onto his lap with my legs on both sides on him. He placed his face in my neck, taking a deep breath. His lips touched my neck like little feather kisses, from the back of my ear down to my collarbone. I felt him pull his face away from me and pulled my shirt off me and threw it somewhere in the room. He placed his left hand behind my back pulling me closer, and his right hand ran over my mark—the black wolf with his name under it. I got tingles all down my spine and a moan coming out of my lips. I heard a groan and looked up to his eyes. He was staring at the wolf with happiness in his eyes. Slowly he leaned down to my mark, brushing his lips over it before kissing it. I threw my head back as pleasure rushed through me like I had never felt before.

"Asher, please," I begged.

However, I had no idea what I was begging for. Asher looked up at me in the eyes, pulling me closer.

"I love you, Willow, always."

I smiled at him and kissed him with all the passion I felt for him.

CHAPTER

I woke up the next morning and slowly made my way to the bathroom. My body was killing me from using it in ways I never knew could happen. I stood in front of the mirror looking at myself. My eyes were brighter than normal. My skin had a glow to it. It looked like I changed everything about myself last night. I looked at my neck, and there was my mark, shining at me like a happy little puppy. I ran my hand over my mark which made me let out a little moan. I heard a groan from the other room. I chuckled and turned the hot water on. Letting it warm up, I ran a brush through my hair, trying to tame the mess. I slipped into the shower and let the warm water work on my sore muscles.

I stood there with my eyes closed when I got an image into my head about last night. Asher ran his hands down my side before he pulled me close to him by my hips. I had to put my legs on both sides of him and straddle him. He slipped my shirt up and over my head where my breast were in front of his face. They could feel his warm breath on them, which made them get so hard. Asher placed small, featherlike kisses from my collarbone down to my nipple before he took it into his mouth. My head fell back as a moan ripped from my lips.

My eyes flew open, and I saw I was in the shower. What the heck was that? I was washing my hair when another thing popped into my head. My eyes closed as the image of Asher leaning over me came to me. He had one arm to the left of me, leaning on his forearm, and the other was running down the side of my face. I looked up at him with so much love in my eyes. He leaned down and smashed his lips to mine in a passionate kiss, one I had never felt before. His hand slipped down to my nipple as he pinched it between his thumb and finger. My back arched off the bed as a muffled scream was stopped by his kiss. His hand then moved down to my stomach where he rubbed it for a little bit in soft light touches. His hand then went down to my clit, and I held my breath.

My eyes snapped open as I was breathing hard. I had never had thought like this, nor had I had them play through my mind like this either. I heard a laugh coming from the sink. I ripped the shower curtain open and glared at Asher who was standing there naked.

"I'm sorry, but my mind cannot stop thinking about last night," Asher said to me.

I looked at him with puzzlement in my eyes.

"You don't know?"

I shook my head no.

"When wolves mate, they can read each other's minds. They can see what the other wants them to see. We can feel each other's moods. Plus, we can talk to each other in our heads." He smiled at me before I heard his voice in my head. *I love you, Willow.*

I smiled from ear to ear and grabbed him to pull him into the shower with me. He let out a chuckle as he climbed in.

I wrapped my arms around his neck and pecked his lips. "You might have to train me because I didn't know this was possible. Can you do that for me?" I whispered, pulling him closer to me.

"Anything for you, little one."

I smiled at him and laid my head on his chest, just hugging him. He pulled away from me which caused me to frown. He smiled and turned me around, grabbing the bodywash. He soaped up his hands and started at my neck, washing my body. I closed my eyes while I enjoyed the rubdown. My mind went back to last night.

Asher was finally going to take my virginity away. "This is going to hurt, but I will take it slow and take care of you. Just tell me if it is too much."

I placed a kiss on his nose and nodded my head. I felt him rub his manhood on my opening. My body arched off the bed when he hit my clit. I felt him push me back onto the bed. I felt pain like I had never felt before. Tears sprang into my eyes, and one rolled down my cheek before I could stop it. Asher raised his hand and wiped it away before kissing me with a ton of passion. I felt so full. I felt pain. I felt happiness. Asher kept kissing my face and neck trying to wait for the pain to go away. I felt a kiss on my mark that made my back come off the bed and a loud moan to come from my throat.

"Asher, move please. I am ready."

He looked up at me and smiled before he pulled out and slammed back into me.

I heard a growl, and my body was spun around. My eyes snapped open and saw I was back in the shower. Asher had black eyes and was looking at me like I was a meal.

"Little one, you don't need to be taught how to show images because I just saw it all."

I smiled at him as he lifted me off the floor; my legs went around his hips. He backed me up to the wall and slammed his manhood into my sore body. My head slammed back into the wall, but I did not feel it, not when my mate was giving this kind of pleasure.

We were in the shower for an hour before he would let me out to dry and get dressed. Today I was to meet the pack and for them to know me as the Luna. I was freaking out. But I was ready.

CHAPTER

It was around lunch time before we were able to leave the house. Asher just would not let me go. We walked over to the pack house to have lunch with everyone. This scared me, and I was not doing good at hiding my mood from Asher. He grabbed my hand and pulled me close to him. He kissed my forehead and told me to just breathe. So I took a deep breath and slowly let it out.

I can do this.

We walked into the house and heard laughing and talking from down the hall. We followed the voices until we came to a door.

"Willow, breathe. It is not the end of the world, and they will love you like I do. You have made it through way more than this in your life, and you came out stronger. You can do this." He pulled me close and kissed my lips.

I smiled up at him and nodded my head. *Let us do this.*

Asher opened the door and pulled me in by my hand. The room was silent.

Okay, was not expecting that one.

Asher pulled me to a table in the front of the room and stood behind a chair in the middle of it. He pulled to the right of him and placed me behind another chair. He looked up at all the people in this room. There were a lot of people, maybe one hundred or more. He cleared his throat and spoke loud and clear.

"Hello, my pack, I would like you all to meet Willow. She is my mate and your new Luna. I want each of you to say hi to her and tell her your name and rank. She is a sweet and shy lady, but she cares with everything she has. She will be the best Luna we have ever had."

I was blushing by the time he was done talking. He pulled my chair out for me, and I sat down. He then sat next to me. He loaded his plate up with more food than I could ever think about eating. He smiled at me when he raised a bite of bacon to my lips. I smiled at him and took the bite, nipping at his fingers. He let out a small growl at me and told me to behave. I chuckled a little and took a drink. I looked down and saw that I did not have a plate and was not sure what was going on.

I thought hard on Asher, saying the same words several times, *Asher, why do I not have a plate?*

After about the fourth time, he smiled at me and nodded his head letting me know he heard me. "This is our first meal together as mates in front of my pack. It is tradition that the Luna does not have a plate and the Alpha feeds her by his hand. It shows that I will always take care of you and that you are more important than I am."

I nodded my head and smiled at him. He lifted another bite of bacon up. I went to get it when I heard his voice in my head.

Do not bite me, little one. I'm sure you don't want me to take you right here, right now, in front of my whole pack.

I turned bright red and lowered my head in submission to Asher.

He placed the bite in my mouth and smiled at me. This went on for the whole meal, him feeding me bites. We were about half through when the first three people came up to us. It was an older man and woman with a teenage girl. They bowed their heads to Asher but did not even looked at me. I did not like that one bit. Was I a no one?

"Hello, Alpha, glad you made it back home safe and sound," the man said to Asher.

Asher nodded his head at the man but did not say anything to them yet. The lady then showed her neck to him in submission.

What is going on?

The teenage girl was standing there with a glare on her face.

Did she eat a lemon before coming up here?

The teenage girl stepped forward and gave one of those sly smiles to Asher before she leaned on the table to show her breast and grabbed his hand.

"Ashy, why are you not returning my calls? We had so many plans and good times together, and here you are just ignoring me now."

What the heck? Did Asher sleep with this child?

He ripped his hand out of her hold and stood up, making the chair fall behind him. I jumped from the noise.

What is going on?

"You will not touch me. You will not call me Ashy. You will respect me and my mate. We never had anything together. You will behave, all three of you!" His voice boomed over the room.

I jumped and started to shake, afraid of him like this. I had never seen him like this before. I guess he could feel my fear because he laid his hand down on my shoulder, rubbing it. Just his touch made me relax.

"Excuse me, but you said you would marry our daughter by the end of this month, and now you bring this slut into the pack, thinking we would accept her?" the dad yelled at Asher.

Me, being me, already knew you do not yell at the Alpha.

Asher was over the table before I could blink and had the man by the throat. "You dare yell at your alpha? Are you stupid?"

The man's eyes were filled with fear as he shook in the alpha's hands.

Asher's eyes turned black; his wolf was now here. "You will submit to me and my Luna, or you will leave this pack. She is now your Luna, and you will respect her!"

I wanted to put my hands on him to calm him down. I took a step forward when I heard his voice in my head.

Please don't step forward. Please let me do this so I can stand up for my Luna. I need you to stand to my right and hold your head up high and support me. Please, Willow.

I took a step forward to where I was at his right and held my head up high.

The daughter looked at me and glared. "You think, just because you spread your legs, for my Ashy, you think you can be Luna of this pack? We need a wolf as our Luna, not whatever you are. I don't smell a wolf in you."

I glared at her as if she was a fly bothering me. I looked over to Asher to see what he was doing. He had let go of the man and took a step back to where he was right next to me. He took my hand into his and gave it a squeeze.

"THIS IS YOUR LUNA. ANYONE THAT HAS A PROBLEM WITH THAT WILL NEED TO COME SEE ME. THERE WILL BE NO PROBLEM WITH WILLOW AS MY LUNA. SHE IS HERE TO STAY." Asher took a deep breath and looked at the family in front of us. "We are done with this. You will remove yourselves from this room and get your attitude together."

The man glared at me and growled. I felt a presence behind me but did not turn around.

"Asher, is everything okay, or have I caused a big problem for you and your pack?" I tried to whisper to him.

He looked down at me and pulled me into his arms. He kissed the top of my head. I heard a growl and looked up as the teenager jumped at me. The dad grabbed Asher away from me as the teenager landed on top of me. I landed on the ground with her knocking the air out of me. She grabbed my hair and slammed my head into the ground. I growled when my head got dizzy and my eyes saw black spots. I opened my eyes to see the teenage girl on top of me. I growled at her and tried to move my arms.

She laughed out loud at me and pushed me harder into the ground. "Ashy is mine, and I will kill you before I let you have him."

I growled at her and pushed her off me. She looked at me with wide eyes as I got back on to my feet.

"I AM YOUR LUNA. YOU WILL RESPECT ME, OR YOU WILL BE REMOVED FROM THIS PACK!"

She just stood there laughing at me.

I got so mad that my body started to shake. My vision started to get black spots in it.

Willow, please calm down. I do not need you going crazy and killing her right now. We can kill her later but not here in front of everyone.

I took a deep breath and tried to calm down. "I will not hurt one of my pack members, but you need to submit to me."

She looked at me with crazy eyes and jumped at me again. I stepped to the side, and she fell flat on her face. The rest of the pack busted up in laughter.

"You are making a fool of yourself," I said, trying to hide my giggles.

I heard her growl as her clothes started to tear away from her body.

This is not the place for this.

I started to walk away. I thought I could get her outside. I got to the door and turned to look at her. She stood there as her small wolf. She looked weak. I took a step out the door and ran to the front door. I heard her running after me.

I flew to the front door and ripped it open. I shifted into a wolf as I hit the grass. I stood with my head up high waiting on her to get out of the pack house. She hit the front lawn in front of me and stood there with wide eyes. I had no idea why she was looking at me that way. Asher walked out behind her and stopped in his tracks looking at me with wide eyes.

Asher, why are you looking at me like that?

Willow, you are a pure-white wolf. They are nonexistent anymore. Did you pick what you are, or did you just turn into a white wolf?

I looked down at my paws and saw a brilliant white color. How odd.

Willow, my name is Ruth, and I am your wolf. Hello. I heard in my head.

I jumped and looked around to the person talking to me. I heard a giggle in my head.

Willow, I am in your head, you silly goose. I am your wolf, and I would like to take over now and show this teen girl what a real Luna looks like. Can you do that for me? Step back in your head and make space for me.

I closed my eyes and thought of sitting in a small dark area. When I opened my eyes, I just saw darkness. I tried to focus on the little light in front of me. Slowly I was able to see out into the world but knew that I was not in control anymore.

Ruth reached out and grabbed the girl by her throat and lifted her up into the air. "I am your Luna! You will respect me, or you will be hurt. I do not want to hurt you, but I will. Make your choice."

The teenager looked at Ruth and growled at her. How stupid could you be? Here she was with her feet dangling in the air with Ruth's hand around her throat, and she growled at us? I could not believe what I was seeing.

"Really? You want to go that way with this whole thing? I am giving you an out. You should take it!" I heard Ruth growl throughout my head.

I got to say, sitting inside your head watching everything happen is a weird feeling.

I heard a whisper in my mind. *Willow, what is going on? Why are your eyes black? I thought you were a shape-shifter, and they don't have animals inside of them. They just change into what they feel.*

I smiled in my head at Asher and his worry for me.

Asher, I am inside of my wolf right now. Her name is Ruth. I do not know why I have a wolf. I do not know how I got a wolf. But when this girl started saying she was sleeping with you, Ruth popped up, and now here we are. She is in control, and I think she wants to rip this girl's head from her shoulders.

I saw Asher stiffen in his body.

Willow, I don't know what is going on, but we will talk once we get Ruth to calm down. Ruth, hello, I need you to take a deep breath and calm down please. I really don't want my Luna killing a pack member on her first day.

Ruth looked up at Asher and took a deep breath. She agreed with Asher as it would not look good on the first day. Ruth let go of the girl's neck, and she fell to the ground. Ruth took steps until she was standing next to Asher. Asher placed his arm around her waist and pulled her closer to his side, kissing her temple. Ruth started to purr.

Willow, you can come forward now and take over. Asher has calmed me down, and I am good now.

So I pushed myself out of our mind and felt myself have control over my body again.

"Welcome back." I heard in my ear.

I could not help but smile from ear to ear. I loved the way Asher was with me, how much he loved me already.

"Now, we must figure out what we are going to do with you, Nicki. Will you behave and stop spreading lies about me, or will you keep being a problem for my pack? You will respect your Luna and alpha. You and I never slept together. Today is the first time we have even spoken to each other."

I could not help but laugh at that point in time. Asher looked at me with a fake glare.

"As I was saying, we do not have any type of relationship with each other besides alpha and pack member. You will learn your place, or you will be kicked out of the pack. Which is it going to be?"

She stood there with her hands balled into fist on her hips, her left foot tapping the ground, and an ugly glare on her face that would not scare a mouse. That was just sad.

"I am to be your wife. Your Luna. Your parents said I could be it, that your mate died, and I was going to replace her since you were alone for so long. So I am to be your mate. Nothing can stop me from being your mate, not even this thing you are holding on to. I will kill her and take her place."

"You really think I could love someone who killed my mate? You really think that I would get over the death of Willow that fast? You really think you can just come along and take what is mine from me and then I fall for you? You are more messed up than I thought."

I grabbed Asher's hand, trying to calm him down.

"Not only will Asher hate you for killing me, but he would hate you even more for killing the future alpha," I said as I placed a hand on my stomach.

Asher looked at me with big eyes and pulled me into a big old hug. I giggled while he held me. We heard a scream and pulled apart. The girl jumped at us trying to get to me. But Asher blocked her way, and he slammed her into the ground.

"YOU DARE TRY TO HARM YOUR LUNA WHO IS WITH CHILD? YOU WILL DIE NOW. I WILL NOT ALLOW YOU TO KEEP TRYING TO HARM MY NEW FAMILY. GUARDS! TAKE HER TO THE DUGONGS."

They came and got her and dragged her away while she was screaming and kicking. The parents then looked at us and both jumped at the same time. Asher grabbed one by his left hand and the other by his right hand.

Oh man, that was hot as hell.

He held them off the ground, but his head whipped back to me as he took a deep breath.

Hold on, Willow. Let me deal with them before I deal with your needs. I can smell you, and it is so sweet. So please try to control yourself for a little bit longer, Asher said with a growl in my head.

I nodded my head yes, and he turned back to the parents he had in his hands.

"You want to follow in your daughter's footsteps and cause harm to my mate? To my unborn pup? That leads you to the death penalty. Is that what you really want?"

The wife kept her mouth shut but was trying to lean her head to the side in submission. But the man was still fighting. Asher sent the man after his daughter to the dugongs. He let go of the woman and took a step back. She leaned her head to the side to show her neck in submission.

I stepped forward to the lady and saw something in her eyes that I know all too well—abuse.

"Why did you not fight with your husband!" Asher yelled at her.

I grabbed his hand and whispered for him to calm down. He looked down at me with questions in his eyes. I stepped up to the woman and took her hand. I led her over to the chairs. We sat down, and I looked up at Asher as he was still standing there. I patted the seat next to me, and he came and sat down.

"May I talk freely?" asked the lady.

We both nodded our heads and waited for her to talk.

"Stan is not my true mate. I have never met my true mate. I do not know if he is alive or dead. Stan was a friend in high school. He asked me out all the time, and I turned him down all the time. He finally had enough, and he drugged me one night, senior year. He forced himself onto me, and I became pregnant because he mated with me and marked me while I was drugged. I felt a pull to him, so I could not leave him. Plus, I had a baby with him, a little boy. After the boy was born, I tried to leave Stan. I did not want my boy to turn out like him. Stan treated me every day to stay, or he would kill our son. I did not think he would do it, so I ran. He found me three days later, and he killed our son." She stopped to blow her nose as I had tears running down my face. "He brought me back to his pack at that time, and everyone kept asking where our son was. Stan said we were attacked by rouges. He finally had enough and moved to this pack and joined under your father. We were living a quiet life, but I would not have sex with him again, afraid he would kill another child.

"On the night that you became alpha, I took my guard down, and he drugged me again. He got me pregnant with the daughter you saw tonight. So I stayed. But he would beat me every night because I was trying to teach our daughter how to be a lady and how to be respectful of others. But Stan would not have it. He wanted her just like him so that he could get power and money. He wanted the girl to marry you, and then he would have all the power and money he wanted as the Luna's dad. He planned on killing you a year after you guys got married and you got her pregnant. I am so sorry, Alpha, for not telling you this." She broke down in tears.

Asher looked like he was in shock.

I reached out and took her hand. "You have nothing to be sorry for. You were being abused. You were being raped. You were being drugged. You watched your son die at the hands of your mate. You have nothing to be sorry for. You did right. You did not keep trying

to hurt me tonight. You stood back with your head to the side showing your neck. You did not want to do all the crap they were trying to
get you to do. And now you come clean about it all. You did good."

Asher nodded his head and agreed with me, and that was how
it was supposed to be.

CHAPTER

It had been several months since I became the Luna of Asher's pack. I was now four months pregnant and only had two more to go. I could hardly wait to hold my little pup in my arms. To see Asher hold them in his big arms just warmed my heart. I could feel that Asher felt the same way. I felt like he had been avoiding me for some reason. I could not get him to talk to me about what was going on. I had tried several ways to get him to talk to me, but all I got was the cold shoulder from him. Right now, I was sitting outside under a willow tree with my feet in the little pond under it. I had my hand resting on my tummy, running small circles around my pup.

"I am going to be the best momma I know how to be. I will not hurt you in any way. My life will come second to you. You will always be first in my life next to Asher."

I heard a twig snap to the side of me, making me jump. I tried to see what was there, but all I saw were shadows. I tried to contact Asher in my head, but it just made my head hurt.

"Aw, so sorry, Luna, but you will not be able to talk to anyone in your head right now." I heard to the other side of me.

My head whipped around so fast I was afraid I was going to break my neck. Someone I did not know was standing there smiling at me.

"Who are you?" I asked.

"I am here to deliver you to your true mate," he said with an evil smile.

I took a deep breath and closed my eyes. *Please, Asher, hear me! I am being taken. I am in the valley under the willow tree.*

I let out a breath and rose to my feet. I took small steps to him, trying to slow down time for Asher to know that there was someone in the territory who was not allowed. I felt him grab my arm and jerk me to him.

"Hurry up, will you. We have a long drive ahead of us."

I closed my eyes and tried to center myself. I tried to move away from the man, but he had a strong grip on me and smelled like rotten fish. My pregnant stomach was trying to hold on to itself. But it was not working well.

I opened my eyes to see that I had thrown up all over the guy. He stepped back from me with a loud growl. He pushed me up against a tree while pulling a rope out of his pocket. He jumped into the pond and started to wash himself off.

With him busy with that, I tried again to reach Asher. *Asher! Please hear me! I am being taken away to David. I am outside at the willow tree by the pond. Please, Asher, I am scared.*

I did not hear anything back. I hung my head down knowing I was not going to get through to him. He has been so closed off to me, blocking his mind from me anymore.

My head shot up fast as I thought of Eric. *Eric! Can you hear me?*

It was quiet for a little bit before I heard him in my head.

Willow, there is an unknown wolf in the area. I need you to go back to the pack house now if you are not already there.

"*Oh, thank goodness, I got ahold of you! I am out at the willow tree by the pond in the valley. I am tied to a tree. The guy is trying to take me back to David. I threw up on him, and he is in the pond washing off. Please hurry.*

It was quiet after that, and I had no idea if he got it or not. I closed my eyes praying that Eric heard my pleas. I heard a twig snap again, and I looked up to see the man standing over me again dripping wet. I let out a little chuckle, not helping myself. He pulled out a knife, and I shut up fast. He cut the rope next to my arm and ended up slicing my arm at the same time. I let out a little whimper.

He laughed at me. "Maybe next time, you will not laugh at the man holding your life in his hands. I would hate for something to happen to that pup in your stomach."

My eyes closed as I heard Ruth let out a growl. I opened my eyes to see him smiling at me again in his evil ways. He grabbed my arm and started to pull me toward a truck that was beaten up. He pulled the door open and pushed me inside of it. I tried to fight him until I felt something poke my back.

"Keep that up, and I will push this knife all the way in."

I stopped in my tracks and slowly climbed into the truck. As he was getting ready to close the door, I heard a loud growl coming toward us—Asher. I could finally breathe knowing my Asher had come for me.

"ASHER! HELP!" I screamed at the top of my lungs.

I felt a hand across my cheek, and my head hit the window behind the seat of the cab. I opened my eyes and looked out of the window.

I saw Asher leap through the air and land on the man trying to take me. The man changed into his wolf, and the guys started to fight, ripping at each other anywhere that they could. There was so much blood, and I did not know which was Asher's and which was the man's. I prayed I could get out of here and not be taken by this man. I watched as Asher sunk his teeth into the man's neck. I heard the door open behind me and let out a scream.

"Be quiet, Willow. It is me, Eric."

I looked up and let out a breath and jumped into his arms.

"Come on. Let's get out of here."

He pulled me into his arms and started to run away. I pulled myself closer to him to keep from bouncing so much.

"I got you, Willow. You are safe with me," he said as he pulled me even closer to him.

My body started to relax being in my friend's arms. Slowly I fell asleep.

I remembered hearing a door close. I remembered going up some stairs. I remembered hearing another door close. I remembered being placed on a bed. I remembered Eric kissing my forehead. I remembered a door closing again. That was the last thing I could remember before I fell into a deep sleep.

I opened my eyes and looked around. I was lying in a field of wildflowers. I sat up to see if I was alone or not. Sitting next to me was a woman all dressed in white.

"Hello, Willow, I am the Moon Goddess, and I am here to have a chat with you. Your baby is going to be an all-powerful being and will rule the werewolves. He will be looked for and tried to be killed by all walks of life. You need to protect your pup with your whole being."

I sat there just staring at this lady. "How could my baby be that important?"

"I want you to do something for me when you wake up. I want you to look up who you really are. You are not the child of those horrible people. You are especially important, and you were stolen. No matter what they told you, it was a lie. You are the most important person right now. The pup in you will keep you safe, but once the pup is out, you will have to keep them safe. Remember what I have told you, child. Do your research. Your parents were especially important. Find them."

I sat up straight in bed breathing hard, trying to find my center. Did that just happen?

CHAPTER

I sat up in bed and looked around the dark room. I was alone. No Asher. I hung my head down and took a deep breath when I heard a voice from the chair on the left side of the room, making me jump.

"Are you okay, Willow?" came Eric's low voice.

I turned my head toward him and let out a small smile.

"I have been worried about you all night. You have been screaming in your sleep."

"I have? I am okay. Just a lot of bad dreams about that guy taking me. Who was he?"

Eric let out a deep breath before he spoke. "His name is Patrick. He works for David and came to take you back to him. How he knows you are alive, we are not sure. With everything that the elder did, he should believe you are dead. Asher has been looking into it and trying to figure it out."

"Is that where he is now?" I said in a small voice, feeling like Asher does not care about me.

"Yes, he is. I am sorry he is not here with you," Eric said as he stood up and made his way to the door.

"Wait," I stopped and cleared my voice. "I mean, please do not leave me right now. I am scared to be alone. With all the bad dreams and that guy fresh in my mind, I do not want to be alone right now. Please, Eric, stay."

Eric looked at me for a long time standing next to the door before he nodded his head and went back to the chair.

"I am sorry you are going through all of this, Willow. I wish there were something I could do to make it all better." I heard Eric whisper.

I smiled at him and then lay back down. After a few minutes, I fell back asleep. Before long, I felt someone shaking me.

"Willow, please wake up. It is just a dream. Willow, wake up." I heard yelling next to me.

My eyes slammed open, and I was looking into Eric's mossy-green eyes. I took a deep breath and reached my arms out to him, placing them around his neck, pulling him closer to me. I started to cry as I laid my head on his shoulder. I felt him rubbing my back.

"It is okay, Willow. I got you."

"Thank you, Eric. Thank you for being here for me. Thank you for keeping me safe. I am glad that I have a friend like you." I sniffled on his shoulder.

"You are more than a friend to me, Willow. You are my Luna, my friend, my sister, my best of the best in everything. I love you so much."

I pulled away to look at him with so many questions going through my head. "What do you mean? Are you in love with me?"

My heart was beating fast in fear that he would say yes. I could not have someone in love with me that was not my mate.

"Oh, no. I love you like a sister. I feel this pull to you like I need to protect you at all cost. That if I lost you, I would lose my sister and her pup. I do not know why I feel this way, but I do."

I let out a breath I did not know I was holding.

I smiled up at Eric and pulled him into another hug. "I feel the same way. I feel safe with you, like you are my brother. I can calm down around you better then I even can with Asher. I do not understand why. I was stolen as a baby and raised by abusive parents. I am going to try to find my real family and see where I came from."

I smiled up at him. Eric placed his hands on the side of my face and pulled me into him as he placed a kiss on my forehead.

The door slammed open and a loud growl was heard. Eric jumped away from me as fast as he could. Asher came charging into the room and had Eric pinned to the wall by his throat.

"Asher, it is not what it looked like. Please let go of Eric and let us explain it to you. Please," I cried, pulling on his arm.

Asher tried to shake me off, but I kept a tight grip on him. Asher looked down at me with nothing but hate in his eyes as he pushed me off him. I fell to the ground wrapping my arms around my pup. I hit the ground hard enough to knock the air out of me but was able to keep my pup safe. I looked up at Asher with tears in my eyes. Eric looked shocked at first and then ticked off.

Eric grabbed Asher's arm and twisted him around to where Asher slammed into the wall chest first. I heard a growl and looked up at the guys.

"You dumbass! You need to calm down so we can explain things to you. There is no reason to throw Willow across the room. There is no reason to hurt her or your pup that way. Now I am going to let go of you, and you are going to sit your ass down in the chair and hear us out."

Asher nodded his head, and Eric let go of him and stepped back.

Asher made his way to the chair by him with his head down. He would not even look at me. Eric came over and helped me up off the ground. When he touched me, I heard a low growl from Asher. Eric helped me to the other chair across from Asher. Eric checked me to see if anything was broken. He nodded his head at me and pulled another chair over to us.

"Now, Asher, let us explain what you saw. I will start with myself, and then Willow can talk."

Asher nodded his head but kept it down.

"I have known Willow even before you found her as a puppy."

Asher's head snapped up with wide eyes.

"Do you remember me telling you the little fox that stole from me and I chased it into a tree hole, the fox disappeared, and a spider jumped on me, making me freak out?"

Asher nodded his head again. What I would not give to hear his voice again.

"That was Willow. That is how I knew she was not a real puppy that night at your house. I smelled her, and she smelled just like that fox. I was terribly upset at her for staying with you in puppy form, and then after that, I could not get past the feeling that she was using you. But as time went on, my feeling for her changed."

Asher let out a loud growl, and Eric slammed his hand down on the arm of the chair.

"Pull your head out of your ass and listen to me, dammit."

Asher lowered his head in shame and nodded his head again.

Eric took a deep breath. "I have been feeling a pull toward Willow that I could not explain. The night that the stupid teenager went after Willow, I want to rip her head off her shoulders. I could not figure out why I had this pull to my best friend's girl, and it scared the crap out of me. So I have stayed away trying to figure it all out. The more I was away from Willow, the stronger the pull got. It was so bad that I slept in front of you guys' door at night just to keep guard, knowing that I would wake up if someone tried to get in. I finally had enough and went to a seer."

Eric hung his head down after saying those words. A seer was a bad person in the land of werewolves. They tried to hunt us all down and kill us.

"She told me that my feelings for Willow are normal for a brother and sister, that maybe we are related and we do not know it. So after a couple weeks, I called my mom and talked to her. I told her all about Willow and how I was feeling toward her. My mom broke down in tears telling me about her past. You see, my mom was raped one night coming home from work. She was bit while at it. She never felt any pull toward the man who did this to her because she already had a mate and was mated to him. After about two weeks, Mom started to feel sick and was throwing up every night. She saw a doctor and found out she was pregnant. She carried the pup until birth. When the baby came out, she knew she was not a werewolf. My mom tried to hide her from the pack. She tried to keep the baby safe and loved her with all her heart."

Eric looked at me and took my hand in his. He then took Asher's hand also. "Asher, this pull toward Willow is because my mom and I think that Willow is my sister who was stolen by a seer when she was only five weeks old."

My breath left me as I remembered my dream with the Moon Goddess. Well, crap.

CHAPTER

It had been about a week since I learned that Eric might be my brother. I did not want to jump right into it. I could have taken a DNA test with him and know the truth right away, but I was afraid that it would come back as maybe he was not my brother since we do not share a dad. I remembered what my parents told me, that I was dropped off at a fire station when I was four weeks old, then spent two weeks in an orphanage. From what Eric said, his sister was stolen at five weeks old. The stories were not adding up together, and I was afraid to get my hopes up. So here I was sitting in the library going through all the old books of people. I had found several families that had lost their children in wars. My heart was breaking for those families; I would break if anything happened to my pup. I placed my hand on my pup, rubbing them. I never want to face losing my pup. A small tear slipped from my eye before I could stop it.

I closed the book and placed it to the side and reached for a new book. This one had several other packs in it. I knew I would see a lot more of heartbreak, but I had to keep moving forward. This was what I had been doing for the last couple of weeks. I wanted to find my family before my pup came. Eric had come and gone checking up on me and helping when he can. He tried to have me read the book his family was in, but I was leaving it to last. People might think I am crazy, but I am not. I was not ready to find out if all my life had been a lie. I was not sure how my pregnant self would handle that. Asher had been avoiding me, and it was driving me crazy. He is my mate. He should be right by me protecting me and our pup.

I did not know what was going on with him, and that broke my heart. I felt like I should have never chosen him as my mate. How could a mate do this to his partner? And pregnant at that. It was not fair. But I could not think about that; otherwise, I would never get out of bed. I needed to find my family. I placed down the next book. It was of no use, just a bunch of older people living in a pack of their own. Any deaths in that was from old age. I picked up the next book, and goose bumps covered my body. I flipped open the old leather book. The very first page told me it was a book of royals. No way was I in this book. I went to put it down, but a voice in my ear told me to look at it. So I slowly flipped through each page.

It started at the 1900s with the first royal family. They were voted in by the werewolf families. It went through each new king and queen and their children. I saw some names along the way that I learned about in school. I saw that the children were killed by war, by love, and by their own parents. I could not believe what I saw when I saw that one king killed his son. His son was going to kill him so he could take the crown, and the king beat him to it. He then gave his crown to the next down son. It broke my heart that a dad could do that to his son. I flipped to the last couple of pages.

This family was named Denver. That was when the goose bumps started. I went on to read.

The Denver family have been king and queen for fifty years now. The king is from a pack to the north. The queen is of royal blood by birth as the niece to the last king. For that king and queen could not have any children. The king is Steven, and the queen is Autumn. The queen had three children together: Eric, Chris, and Callie. Eric did not want to be king, so he stepped down and became beta of a south pack. Chris is to take over the crown. Callie is yet to find her mate currently. The queen was attacked by a man whom no one knows. She became pregnant from that. She gave birth to a girl whom they named Willow. When Willow was four weeks old, she was stolen from the home. They have yet to find her. The king and queen have looked high and low for their daughter with no luck of finding her.

Okay, so I had no reason to doubt that Eric was my brother.

Eric, are you there?

Always. What can I do for you, Willow?

I would like to take the DNA test please. I know there is a chance that we do not fully add up because of whoever my dad is. I think we might because of having the same mom. I will take the chance now.

"Okay, do you want to do it now? I am not busy. I can meet you downstairs."

"Okay, see you in about five minutes."

I took a deep breath and cleaned up the mess I had made in the library. After I was done, I cleaned my hands and headed downstairs. Eric was standing at the bottom waiting for me. When I got close enough, he grabbed me and pulled me into a hug. I felt safe and warm in his arms. All fear left me as I took in his smell, like oranges and pinecones. He pulled back from me and took my hand, leading me to the basement where the hospital and doctors' offices are. When we got down there, he walked over to a desk where a pretty lady was sitting. She looked up at Eric and smiled brightly. She then looked at me and glared at me.

"Whoa, Kim, do not glare at your Luna. You might end up in the basement like the other people," Eric said with a laugh.

She hung her head, showing her neck to me. "Forgive me, Luna. I forgot."

I smiled at her. "That is okay. I would, however, like to have a test done please."

She smiled big at me, showing most of her bright white teeth. "Oh, what kind of test can we do for you?"

Eric then spoke up for us, "We would like to have a DNA test done. I would like to know if our new Luna is my sister."

She nodded her head and picked up the phone to talk to someone.

"Please have a seat. Dr. Greene will be out in just a little bit to get you."

We said our thank you and went to sit down. My mind was going ninety to nothing. I could not stop thinking about if I was royalty, if I had several brothers and sisters. My head snapped up when

I heard our name called. We went into a small room and sat down in some chairs. The doctor walked in behind us.

"Hello, Luna, Eric. So I hear that you two want a DNA test. Is that true?"

I was shaking so much that Eric took my hand to calm me down and spoke for us. "Yes, we think we are brother and sister. We have a pull to each other, and I want to protect her over everything. But it is not a mate pull."

We had blood drawn and our cheeks swabbed. Then the doctor told us it would be about forty-eight hours before he knew if we are related. That was a long time to sit with my thoughts.

I spent a lot of time in the library reading about my maybe family. I took walks outside with Eric. He told me about his childhood, why he gave up the crown, and his relationship with his parents and brother. He did not talk much about Callie. When I asked, he just brushed it off. I was about to go insane when we got the call to head back to the doctor.

Eric and I were sitting in the hard chairs again waiting for the doctor to come in. It felt like a lifetime before he came in.

"Welcome back, guys. The test is back, and they say that you guys are 80 percent related. If I were you, I would get your mom to come in and have a test with her to see if the percentage goes up. That is the only way to know 100 percent if it is brother and sister."

We thanked him and went back upstairs.

"I am going to call my mom and tell her what we have found out."

I nodded my head and went up to my room. I took a hot shower, changed into warmer sleepwear, and crawled into bed closing my eyes.

Over the next couple of weeks, not much had happened. Asher was still avoiding me. I had no clue what I did, but my pregnancy was taking its toll on me. I had been sick for weeks on end, and I could not stop being sick. I hugged the toilet day in and day out. I could not keep anything inside of me. I was right now lying on the floor of our bathroom—well, mine now since Asher had not slept in our room in three weeks. My heart was breaking. I did not know what I did, and he just shut me out. There had been no more threats from David, that I knew about. I am a broken person now. My head was lying on my hands as tears rolled down my flushed cheeks. I heard the bathroom door open but paid no attention to it. I felt warm hands on my ice-cold arms and lifted my eyes to see who it was. Of course, it was Eric. Not that I was mad at it, but it was always Eric.

"Willow, please let me take you to the doctor. This is not normal for a she-wolf to suffer like this with a pup. Please."

I nodded my head at Eric the best I could. I felt myself being lifted into his arms. He pulled me close to his warm chest. I pushed myself closer to him to feel the heat on my cold body. My head started to spin with how fast he is walking to the doctor's office. My head started to feel heavy, so I just let it drop down his arm. My arms went weak, and they just hung off him. I bet I looked like a dead person lying in his arms with my pup belly showing. I felt Eric hurry up as I started to doze off.

"Please help our Luna. I found her in the bathroom like this lying on the floor." I heard his worried voice.

I was placed onto a table. My clothes were stripped off me, and a night gown replaced them. I felt a sharp pain in my arm which I guessed was the IV. I lay there going in and out. I remembered them checking me out. I remembered my pup being checked. I remembered Eric yelling at the doctor. I remembered the doctor yelling to get Asher. I remembered the nurse saying Asher would not come. I remembered them saying that Asher did not think the pup was his, that he thought it was Eric's. I remembered Eric growling so loud and running out of the room. Other than that, I did not remember anything.

I woke up to a bright room. My eyes burned from the brightness of it. I snapped my eyes close fast. I heard someone move around the room and then heard a small voice.

"You can open your eyes now."

I reopened them and looked around. I saw a small woman sitting in a chair by my bed.

"Hello, my name is Autumn. I am your mother."

My breath hitched in my throat. How did she know that?

"You are wondering how I know that. Well, while you were out, we did a blood test. It came back 99.9 percent that I am your mom. So Eric is your brother." She smiled at me while I broke down in tears. "Oh, sweetheart, it is okay. I am here now. I will be with you every step of the way."

"Hi, I am Willow."

"Oh, honey, I know who you are. I am so glad that we were able to find you again. It had been a long time. You have grown up into a pretty woman."

I smiled at her and reached my hand out to her. She pushed my hand away and wrapped me in a tight hug. I busted out laughing.

"We have a lot to talk about, and we will do that as we go. But right now, we must pull your mate's head out of his ass. You are sick because of him. He has pulled himself away from you, and it is making your pup suffer. We will fix it all up. Eric is talking to him right now, telling him that I am your mother and he is your brother, that you two never had sex, and that the pup is not his. It is up to you if you let him back in after he learns the truth. I, however, would have a hard time letting him back in after not trusting you. But that is for you to figure out." She smiled at me with an evil look in her eyes, like she had been through something like this before and knew just what to do.

There was a knock on the door, and she stepped away from me to answer it.

"Hello, Asher, what can I do for you?"

"I would like to see Willow."

"Well, that is up to her. Willow, would you like to see Asher?" She winked at me while asking me that.

I smiled at her and winked back and nodded my head. I saw her nod back and open the door for him. He came in with his head hung low. He had a bruise on his cheek and on his eye. Looked like Eric took his anger out on him. He walked closer to me with small steps.

"Willow, I am so sorry for everything that I have done to you. I never meant to hurt you or our pup. I am so deeply sorry."

I turned my back to Asher and looked out the window. I had tears running down my cheeks and could not let him see that.

"Willow, please look at me. I am so sorry."

I did not turn around.

"Asher, I cannot look at your right now. I cannot let you back into my life that quick. I cannot let you back in with you knowing what you have done to me. To think that I would cheat on you with my own brother. To not listen to me or Eric no matter how many times we told you it is not true. To shut off the link between us, to not hear me call for help, and not to know what I am feeling. What I am going through. No, I will not let you right back in. You must earn the right to be my mate again, to be the father of this pup. You have a lot of work to do and extraordinarily little time to do it in. If I were you, I would get to work fast. Now leave."

I heard him let out a breath and walk to the door.

"Please, Queen Autumn, take good care of her. She does mean the world to me," came his broken voice.

I almost took back everything I said when I heard it. But Autumn's voice stopped me.

BIRTH OF THE CHOSEN ONE

"You, my son, have a lot of work to do to win back your mate and pup. You need to treat her like she is the queen in your life, that nothing comes before her, that you would die for her. And right now, you are not acting that way. You are broken for, what, twenty-four hours? She has been broken for three months. Get your act together and know what it feels like for what you did to her. Turn the link back on and feel the way she feels. But do it behind closed doors because you do not want the pack to see what you have done to their Luna through that link." Then she closed the door in his face. She came back over to me and sat down, picking up my hand. "It will be all okay soon."

I spent three days with Autumn, learning about my family—all the people in the family and everyone who meant anything to them. It was a lot to take in, so I asked Autumn to give me a break today so I had time to think for myself. I was lying in bed talking to my pup when the door opened. In walked a man I had never seen before.

"Hello, how can I help you?" I asked, almost afraid to speak.

"I am here to take you for a drive. It is better to get out into some fresh air," came his gruff voice.

It sent shills down my neck.

"Who sent you here to get me?" I asked, backing up in the bed reaching for the nurse button.

He made fast work of getting to me before I could push the button.

"I would not do that if I were you. They do not want you to go out, but your brother Eric thinks it would be good for you to get fresh air," came his quick reply.

I nodded my head and started to get out of bed.

"Here, let me carry you. That way, we do not strain your legs trying to hide from the nurses."

My mind was going around and around knowing something was not right. I did not want to cause him any reason to know that I was uncomfortable with him. He leaned down to pick me up, and I smelled smoke and beer on his clothes. I wrapped my arm around his neck.

"I need you to lay your head down so the nurses do not see your face. Can you do that for me please?" he asked.

So I did. This gave me a chance to open my mind-link and contact Eric.

Eric, are you there? There is a man here to take me for a drive, and he said that you sent him. He even called you my brother. I have no clue who this guy is and how he knows that you are my brother. I did not know we were telling people yet.

I waited and waited but heard nothing back from him. We were now getting close to the car, and I had to try one more person.

So I reached out to Autumn. *Mom, did Eric send someone to take me for a car ride?*

The answer came back fast.

What? No. Do not go with that man!

I looked up as the guy placed me inside of the car.

Mom, too late. He carried me out of the hospital. He has now placed me inside of the back of a red car. Please, help me.

I heard nothing else after that. The man got into the car, looked back at me and smiled, then took off fast. I grabbed the seat belt and slapped it onto me fast. My body felt it as we crossed the territory line. The car zipped around the curves and hills of the outer road, speeding away from my home.

"Just lay your head back and take a nap. It is a long drive to get to where we are going."

I let out a sigh and thought of how to word my question.

"Can you be so kind as to tell me where you are taking me, please?"

He looked at me through the mirror with one eyebrow raised.

"I am taking you back to your parents."

"Which parents would that be?"

He looked at me with a question in his eyes. "Your mom and dad. You only have one set of parents."

"Well, I have two sets. One is my birth mom and dad, Steven and Autumn, and second set is Tammy and Mike, who stole me from my real parents."

The car came to a quick stop, squealing the tires. My seat belt cut into my shoulder.

"What do you mean stole you?"

"I was five weeks old when they broke into our home and took me out of my bed. They said my mom did not want me and left me at a fire station. They beat me and abused me for years until I ran away at sixteen." I watched as his eyes widened. "Okay, what is going on in your head?"

"Do you know where you were?" he asked me.

I nodded my head.

"You know you were in a werewolf hospital?"

Again, I nodded my head.

"You know that you are human right?"

I looked at him, confused.

"No, I am not human. That is how I knew those people were not my real parents."

He just looked at me really confused now. He nodded his head and started to drive again. A little bit later, he pulled over at a hotel.

"Please, behave for me. I am not taking you to those people, but I do need to get some answers, and here is the best place to do that."

I nodded my head. We both got out of the car and headed inside. We walked up to the counter, and a nasty-looking woman walked up to help us. She looked at this man with lust in her eyes. I thought she should be out on the street trying to get guys to buy her for the hour. Her skirt was showing her butt cheeks. Her makeup was caked on.

The man placed his arm around my waist and pulled me closer to him. "Do you have a room for my wife and me? She is pregnant and cannot take long hours in the car anymore."

I looked up at him with wide eyes while he smiled down at me. She nodded her head and started to tap on the keyboard.

"Yes, I have one, but if you get bored tonight with someone so fat and ugly, you can come find me down here, sexy."

I rolled my eyes at her while she glared at me. The guy took the key and pulled me from the room.

"Sorry about that. It happens everywhere I go," he said to me.

I just shrugged my shoulders. Like I really care. We got to the room, and he opened the door. It was kind of dingy. Had a bathroom, couch, and a king-size bed.

"You will sleep on the bed, and I will take the couch. But first I want to talk to you."

I nodded my head once again. We sat down on the couch with him to my right.

"Can you start with how you knew where you were?"

I let out a deep breath and looked at him. "First tell me how you knew that was a werewolf hospital."

He nodded his head and took a deep breath also.

"Well, since we both know about werewolves, I can tell you I am one myself. I am from a different pack than that one, but my pack is in the same town that your 'parents' live in."

I laughed at that one.

"Well, I am a shape-shifter. That is how I knew they were not my parents. See, my mom was raped, so my dad is someone I do not know. But my mom is a werewolf. She has been helping me while I was in the hospital."

"Do you want to tell me why you were in the hospital?"

I shook my head no; he did not push it.

"Okay, so you know who your real mom is?"

I nodded my head.

"If you were in a werewolf hospital, that means that you are mated to a werewolf, right?"

Again, I nodded my head yes.

"Will you tell me who it is?"

I so hoped that he did not keep me, knowing how important I was now.

"I am mated to the alpha of that pack. I am the Luna." I held my breath while the wheels turned in his head.

"OH SHIT! Are you saying that I just kidnapped the Luna of a pack? Of the most feared pack there is?" he asked me as he began to shake.

I just nodded my head. He took some deep breaths.

"It gets worse if you ask me," I said to him.

He looked up at me with wide eyes. I could see the fear in his face.

"My mom, that you took me away from, is the Queen Autumn. My dad is King Steven."

At this point in time, his face was washed of all color. He looked at me with wide eyes, not even breathing. Next thing I knew, he was on the ground passed out. Well that went well.

CHAPTER

The next day, I woke up to an empty room. I took a nice hot shower. I stood there for a little bit just letting the warm water run down my pregnant belly. My mind was empty while in the shower, just enjoying it. I could worry about getting home after I got out. After my fingers started to prune, I got out and dried off. I walked over to the counter and saw a bag of clothes. I pulled the stuff out and found leggings and an oversized shirt. I slipped them on and walked out of the room. I was surprised to see the man sitting on the couch with food placed in front of him.

"Come, eat. Feed that pup of yours." He patted the seat next to him.

Did not have to tell me twice. I sat down and dug into all the food in front of me.

"We got off to a bad start yesterday. I'm Parker."

"Hello, I'm Willow." I smiled at him.

"I am taking you back home today. Please, let them know it was a mistake and that I am sorry before we get back. I do not want to end up dead today," he told me with a shake in his voice.

I patted his back.

"I got you, Parker."

He smiled at me while we finished eating. After about an hour, we had checked out of the hotel and was heading back again, this time with me in the front seat.

"Parker, I am going to talk to them now."

He nodded at me while I slipped into a mind-link.

Hello, Eric, are you there? I waited for a little bit but got nothing back from him. So I went to the next person. *Hello, Mom, are you there?*

"*Oh my gosh, Willow, where are you?* came her reply.

Leave it to my mom to answer me on the spot.

I am heading back. The guy I am with is named Parker. He was hired to kidnap me by the people who stole me. When he found out who I was and the truth, he said he would bring me back. I want no harm to come to him. He was lied to like I was. But now we are heading back.

I will do what I can. I am the queen, so it should not be too hard, she said with a laugh.

Thank you, Mom.

I cut the mind-link and looked over at Parker. He smiled at me and moved on with the trip. We talked here and there, just small talk. Before I knew it, we were back at the pack's line. Parker pulled the car to a stop. I saw sweat running down his brow.

"Hey, it will be okay."

He smiled a small smile and opened the car door. Before I knew it, he was on the ground with a wolf standing over him. Parker was not fighting back at all.

"HEY! GET OFF OF HIM NOW!" I commanded.

The wolf jumped off him. The wolf looked at me, then ran to the trees. Moments later, Jason came walking back out. I breathed a sigh of relief.

"Jason, why did you attack Parker?"

"Luna, I have orders to get him back to the pack house and take him to the cells."

I hung my head in shame.

"Who ordered you to do that?"

"The alpha did."

"Did the queen not say to leave this man unarmed?"

"She did, but the alpha does not care. He took you, so he should pay the price."

I shook my head. How could I have fallen for this man?

"Parker, get up."

He climbed up to his feet and stood there just looking at me.

"I thank you for not taking me the people who stole me and beat me. I am afraid others are not seeing it that way. So you are free to go. Get into your car and drive away. Jason here will see me to the pack house where I will explain it all. I do not want you getting hurt because of me. You have protected me and brought me back. I will forever be grateful and always remember you. Thank you." I then gave him a hug and sent him on his way.

Jason stood there with is mouth hung open. I just looked at him and shook my head. Then Jason ran into the trees again. A couple of minutes later, he came back out as his wolf. He kneeled next to me for me to climb up on his back.

"Are you kidding me, Jason? I will break your back with all this pup weight. I cannot even see my feet anymore."

Jason let out a little growl at me, and I sighed.

"Fine, if I break your back, that is on you." And I slowly climbed on. I grabbed his fur as he took off running. "Jason! Slow down, buddy. I cannot handle all the bouncing."

He slowed down to where it was a nice trot.

We came to a stop in front of the pack house. Standing there was Eric, Autumn, Steven, and Asher. Everyone looked happy to see me but Asher. He just looked ticked off like normal. Eric stepped forward and helped me off Jason. I patted his back as he took off back to his post.

"Willow, I am so glad you are okay!" came a happy and big hug from Eric.

"Why did you not answer any of my mind-links?" I asked, feeling really hurt.

Eric hung his head. "I was not allowed to answer you. I was forbidden from doing it. And I cannot go against the alpha's orders."

Now that really hurt.

"Willow, my child, I am so glad you are back. I am never going to leave your side again," came my mom as she also pulled me into a big hug.

I smiled back at her and hugged just as tight.

"Willow, I may not be your true father, but I would love to try to become the dad you want. Would you let me?" asked Steven.

I turned to look at him with wide eyes.

"Yes, yes, yes," I cried as I jumped into his arms in a bear hug.

He laughed as he hugged back just as tight. When we pulled away, I looked over at Asher.

"You got anything to say to me, Asher?"

He just looked at me with dead eyes.

"No, you mean nothing to me, and when my pup comes out, you will not be worth anything."

I hung my head crying. Asher turned around and walked away with my family yelling at him.

"Let's get you inside, and we can talk about a bunch of things," said my mom.

I followed with my head still down. We went into a room I have never seen before.

"Have a seat, hon. We have to talk."

I sat down and looked around the room. The walls were bare, and only three chairs in the room.

"What kind of a room is this?" I asked.

Autumn looked at Eric and nodded her head. He stepped out of the room closing the door.

"This room is made from silver. No wolf can hear in. Eric has stepped out because he would have to tell Asher what we talked about if he asked."

I nodded my head and took a deep breath. I looked from my mom to my dad, waiting for them to talk.

"Willow, we want you to come home with us. You can have your pup there and protect them from Asher. We have no idea what is going on with him, but we fear for your life if you stay here. We have belief that Asher is the one that told David and your so-called parents that you are alive. We think you are in danger if you stay here. If you come back with us, we will protect you and your pup," Steven said to me.

I felt a tear roll down my cheek. I sat quiet for a little bit before I spoke up.

"I agree with you both. I will go with you. When do we leave?"

Both let out a breath.

BIRTH OF THE CHOSEN ONE

"We leave in an hour. You need to get anything from your room that you want to take with you."

I nodded my head and got up to hug them both.

"Meet us at the side door off the kitchen in one hour," Steven said to me.

I nodded yet again. We left the room and went our own ways.

I went up to my room and looked around. I could smell another female in the room, so I knew Asher had been cheating on me. This would be easier than I thought. I went to the closet and saw all my clothes were gone. Same as in the bathroom. He really did hate me. I left that room and walked over to the pup's nursery. The room was still the same as I left it. I walked around the room touching everything. I saw the blanket that I bought. It was the first thing I bought for my pup. It was dark green with sloths on it hanging from trees. I pulled it to my body, hugging it. I looked around the room and everything else Asher had someone else buy. He did not even help me buy things for our pup.

I walked out of the room with the blanket in my arms. As I walked past Asher's office, I could hear a woman moaning. Tears filled my eyes as I stood there staring at the door. How could a mate do this to their mate? How could my life lead me to this? I was so over it all. I flung the door open, and there it was. Asher was sitting in his chair leaning back with that teenager riding him. He looked up at me and gave me an evil smile. I just shook my head and walked out of the room, slamming the door behind me. No one should know how that feels. Here I was pregnant with his pup, his mate, and he was cheating on me. Well, no more. He can be stupid; I am out of here.

I walked downstairs and went to the door I was to meet my parents. I waited for about ten minutes before they walked over to me.

"Are you ready?" asked my mom.

I let out a small yes and stepped out the door.

"Where are your bags?"

"Asher removed everything that was mine and moved in another girl's stuff. I have no idea where anything is, and I do not care. All I want to take with me is the blanket that I bought my pup."

We loaded the bags and ourselves into the van and started to drive off. I looked around the van. There was my dad and mom, but what surprised me the most was Eric was here.

"Eric, what are you doing here? You are the beta."

"I will not stay with an alpha that would treat his mate the way he has you. I will no longer serve under him. I will take my place as the second king."

I grabbed his hand into my own, happy that he was coming with us. He smiled down at me.

Willow, where do you think you are going? came Asher in my head.

"Did Asher try to talk to you?" asked Eric.

"Yes, he is trying now. But I do not want to answer him. He was having sex with that teenager when I went to get my stuff."

"It is okay. Turn off the link. He will not be able to get to you. He will feel the tear as soon as we cross the line. We are almost there. He will feel both of us leaving him."

I nodded my head and waited for the tear of our bond.

As we passed the line, I felt my heart start to hurt, but it was short lived because of all the pain I had felt because of him. I heard a loud howl as we drove away from my mate. It sounded like a painful howl, but at this point, I did not care. I was going to live my life with my family.

I, Willow Rose, felt like I was going to die. I was in the last couple of weeks of having my pup, and my body felt like it was going to pop. I was stuck in this room with no one to talk to. I had nowhere to go. No one to see. I thought moving here was going to be great. But, oh, how wrong I was. It all started the second we pulled up into the driveway.

"Willow, I want you to follow me to your room when we come to a stop. Do not talk to anyone or look at them," came Eric's strict voice.

I had never heard him speak that way before. I nodded my head and looked down at the ground. When we came to a stop, I felt a hand on my arm as it yanked me out of the van.

"Come now, Willow. I do not have all day." Once again, it was Eric.

What did I do wrong?

I got out of the van and was following Eric when I felt something tug on my ankle. I looked down, and a woman was on her knees.

"Please, please let me free. I did not do anything wrong." I heard the woman weep.

Eric walked around me and kicked the lady in the stomach.

"Shut up, woman. You know what you did, and you must now pay for it!" he yelled at her.

I jumped back and tried to run away, but Eric grabbed me and picked me up.

"You will behave, Willow. I have too much to do now that we are back. You need to not be a problem for me!" he yelled at me.

Did I step into a warped world? I watched as we climbed the steps and moved my eyes around looking. There were several men and women on their knees cleaning. There were several crawling around to get something. I was so confused right now.

We made it to a room, and Eric walked in and threw me on the bed, making me bounce.

"Be careful of my pup, brother."

Eric just looked at me and laughed.

"Oh, I am not your brother, Willow. We changed the results so you would trust us and come here. You are now going to give birth to this pup here where we can claim it as our own. We will raise them to be the next king or queen. And you will live here forever just watching from far away. You see, my sister cannot have kids. No one wants to give theirs up to her. So we just played you so that we could carry on the name."

I had tears running down my face as he turned and walked away. I sat on that bed for several days just crying.

One week later, I tried to get a hold of Asher, but it was like something was in the way. I could not figure it out. I went to the bathroom to take a shower and saw a big claw tub. So instead, I took off all my jewelry and climbed into here. I was thinking about my pregnant belly when I heard a faint whisper in my ear.

Willow, get rid of the earrings.

I had no clue what was going on. I pulled out one of the earrings to have a look at it and saw that it was not mine. I always had in little green butterflies. These were on a lion. I pulled the other one out and set it on the tub. When did I get these? I did not remember changing my earrings at any time. I sat back in the tub and rested my head on the back, trying to think of when my earrings could have been changed.

Willow? Please, Willow, answer me! came the scared voice of Ruth.

I jumped up to sit up straight.

BIRTH OF THE CHOSEN ONE

Ruth? Where have you been? I have tried to talk to you several times. I almost cried at her.

I have been here the whole time, but those earrings have blocker in them. I could not get to you, and neither could Asher.

I leaned back in the tub thinking of Asher, the man who broke me.

No, no, no. Asher has not broken you. Your so-called family has lied about a lot of things. Asher has been trying to get to you, but they have pushed you guys apart.

What? Why would they do that? I was so confused right now. Then I remembered why I was here—so they can take my pup and raise it as royal however they want. Oh, crap, what was I going to do?

Willow, try to reach Asher. Tell him where we are. We need him to come get us. The pup will be born soon, and I am afraid that after the pup is done being fed by you, they will kill you. We need Asher.

I took a deep breath and thought of Asher, thought of the time we had before all of this happened, and thought of all the laughs and lovemaking.

Willow, you need to stop that right now. It has been way too long for me.

I let out a giggle feeling how horny he is.

Willow, I never thought I would hear from you again.

Asher, why did you sleep with that teenager?

What? I would never cheat on my mate. And with the mate bond, you would have felt if I did.

What do you mean I would have felt it?

I heard Asher let out a sigh before he started to talk again. *Every mate can feel if their mate is being unfaithful to them. It is a burning hard and sharp pain in the stomach. You can feel the ghost of what is going on. Your heart feels like it will rip out of your chest and explode.*

Then why did you think this pup was Eric's if you never felt that with me?

What are you talking about? I would never think my pup is someone else's. I feel the pull to the pup. I can smell my scent on the pup. I never thought our pup was someone else's.

We need to sit down and talk about a lot of things. Things have been said to me that was a lie, and now I have no idea what is right and wrong.

Willow, I need you to listen to me. I love you with all I have. I would never do those things to you. I have tried to get to you since you ended up in the hospital but have not been able to get to you. There has been some force field around you that I could not get through. I have not been able to talk to you or get close to you. I still love you, Willow.

I leaned my head back and just started to cry. All these months had been nothing but lies.

Asher, I need you to find me and fast. They plan on taking our pup and giving it to his sister to raise as her own. I will not be needed after that. I am not their family. They lied and changed the papers so it looked real. They put earrings in my ears that I did not know about, and they are what have blocked us from talking. I have now removed them. They have lied to me about a lot of things. And I am guessing they have lied to you too. I need you to save your pup.

Willow, you hold on until I can get there. I am getting you and our pup. I need you to put the earrings back in. Do not let them know that we know. Every night, take a bath and take them out then. We will talk every night. But we cannot let them know that we are onto them. Can you do that for me?

Yes, Asher, I can do that. I love you.

I love you too, Willow.

I closed my eyes and took deep breaths before I put the earrings back in. I pulled the plug of the tub and dried myself off. Slipping into the nightgown, I headed back into the room. As I entered the room, I stopped in my steps. Sitting on the bed was Callie.

I took a deep breath and got ready for all the lies that would come from her mouth.

"I am sorry for what my family has done to you. No one should be taken like you were. No one should be lied to like that. I have not found my mate yet, and they have made me lie about it. That is why I cannot get pregnant. I do not want your pup. I want to help free you. But you must trust me, and I know that is going to be hard for you. If I know Asher as well I as I think I do, he will come for you.

I will help make sure he can get to you. Please take out the earrings so we can chat."

I looked at her weird but removed the earrings anyway. I felt a new presence in my head.

Hello, Willow, it is Callie. Asher? Are you there?

We waited for a little bit before he finally answered.

Callie, what do you want?

I am here with Willow. Say hi, Willow.

Hello.

Callie, please do not hurt her.

Asher, I would never do that. I want to get her back to you. I do not love my family, and I want to be free also when you come for her. I want to find my mate and live in peace. I do not want to be queen. I want freedom. If you can give me that, I will help free her.

I looked up at Callie with wide eyes. She really hated her family. My mind was blank for a little bit which told me that Asher was thinking.

Callie, you and I have always been friends. Your mate is here in my pack. He found you the last time you were here to visit. He tried to get to you, but your parents locked him in the basement so you could not feel him. If you are true to your words, I will help you both. But Willow and my pup are my first to save.

Callie looked at me and let out a small smile.

You got a deal, Asher. I will help you. I will make sure she is fed and that no harm will come to her. I will contact you tomorrow around lunch time to tell you where we are. That will give me time to figure out where they have hidden us.

Okay, I will talk to you then. Do not cross me, or I will have to kill you with the rest of them.

Deal.

The link closed after that, and I placed my earrings back into my ears. I looked at Callie like she had two heads.

"My family is the worst there is. I will protect you the best that I can. I do promise you that one, Willow. I will never go against Asher. He has always been like a brother to me, more so then my own brother."

After that, she got up and walked out of the room. I heard her lock the door before hearing her walk away. I lay down in bed thinking about everything that just happened. Maybe I could get back to Asher and work through all of this. I prayed I was back before my pup came into this world.

The next day was the longest day of my life. I knew that I got to talk to Asher that night, and it seemed that time just went oh so slow. I was sitting on the window bench when the door opened, causing me to jump. In walked someone who I had never seen. He was a big man with tattoos everywhere, even on his face. He walked over to me without saying a word and picked me up by my hair. The scream I let out of my mouth was one that I had never done before. He picked me up by my arm and threw me onto the bed. He smiled an evil smile that made bile rise in my throat. I tried to get to the headboard of the bed, but with my belly, it made it hard for me to move.

He grabbed my ankle and pulled me back down to him, letting out a chuckle. My skin was crawling, afraid of what was to come. He rubbed his hot, sweaty hand up my leg toward my knee. I flailed my arms around trying to hit him. He pulled me closer to him to where my legs were around his waist. My pulse was going through the roof, and my face was getting hotter and hotter with fear and anger.

How dare he do this to me.

I yelled as loud as I could hoping someone would hear me. For that, he slapped me across the face, making my head turn fast.

I felt the tears rolling down my hot cheeks as I fought this man. He pulled both my knees toward him again and lined himself up with me. This was it. This was the last time I could get free. I let out a bloodcurdling scream as I kicked and flung my arms around. He undid his pants and ripped my underwear off.

Goddess, if you can help me, please send help. I closed my eyes praying someone would save me from this man.

My eyes flew open when I heard the door slam against the wall.

"What do you think you are doing, John?" came Callie's voice. Oh, thank goodness.

"I am teaching her the way of our people," came the man's nasty voice.

"And who told you to do this?" Callie ordered.

"Your parents told me to visit with her."

All this time, he still had not let me go. His hands were still rubbing on my legs, just waiting to get inside of me.

"Let her go now and move on with someone else. She is off-limits while she is pregnant. We do not want anything to happen to the pup if you are too rough. Plus, knowing you, you will be too rough with her."

He let me go and pushed me up the bed with a rough hand. He stomped out of the room and slammed the door behind him. Callie rushed over to me.

"I am so sorry, Willow. I came as soon as I heard what they told him to do." She sat by me and held onto my hand.

"Thank you for saving me."

"You are welcome. Sorry I said he could have you after the pup is born. It was the only way for him not to think that I was saving you," she said with her head bowed.

"I understand."

"Come now. How about shower and new clothes?"

I agreed with her and took a shower. After, I got redressed and sat back by the window. I was alone in the room after the shower and was afraid that I would have another visit from that man. Asher, please hurry.

The rest of the day, I sat in my room trying to think of a way to get out. Nothing that I tried to figure out would work. I might have ran from my parents, but their setup was not like this one. I went to the bathroom and pulled the earrings out. As soon as the second was out, I heard the voice in my head.

Willow, please answer me… I am so worried.

Asher, I am here. It is okay.

Callie told me what happened today. I am so sorry I was not there to protect you.

It is okay, Asher. I know that you would have if you could have. I am okay. Maybe a little bruised up, but nothing that will not heal. He did not hurt me in any other way but hitting me on the cheek.

I am glad you are okay. Callie was able to tell me where you are. Several of my men and I will be there tomorrow. We have been traveling all night. I am coming for you, Willow. Just a little bit longer. It should be around nightfall. Just hold on a little bit longer. I love you, Willow."

I love you too, Asher. We will wait for you. Your pup is ready to meet you.

We closed the link; and I took my shower, changed into a nightgown, and crawled into bed. Today had been a little too much for me. My belly had been hurting all day. I had been cramping and hurting from being manhandled. A nice long sleep was what my body needed right now. I closed my eyes and fell right to sleep, dreaming about my little pup and his dad. I hoped I lived to see my dream of them playing baseball together.

I woke up about three in the morning with my stomach all in knots and ran to the toilet. After I got done being sick, I lay back up against the tub. I had sweat beading up on my forehead and hot all over. My stomach kept flipping around. I pulled the earrings out of my ears and thought of Asher.

Asher, are you awake?

No, but I am now. What is wrong?

I have been sick for a while now, and I am running a fever. I am sweating a lot, and my stomach is cramping horribly bad. I do not know what is wrong with me.

Willow, sit tight. I am going to ask Dr. Greene what might be wrong. I will be right back.

Okay.

I sat for a little bit with my eyes closed when I felt the need to be sick again. I jumped forward and made it to the toilet just in time. What was going on with me? I was worried that somehow my fake parents have made me sick. After what felt like an hour, Asher got back to me.

Willow, we think you are in labor. How far apart are you throwing up?

I have not been timing it.

Okay, I need you to leave your link open, and I will time you, okay?

I will try.

We then started to talk about other things going on to pass the time. I jumped forward and once again threw up. I let out a sigh again and sat back down.

Are you okay, Willow?

Yeah, just sick of being sick.

I am timing now, so do not close the link.

Okay, Asher.

We sat and talked again for a while. I was getting tired and wanted to go back to sleep, but Asher kept me awake as the link would close if I slept. I was telling about my day when I jumped forward again.

You are okay, Willow. I will be right back.

It was quiet in my head while I got sick. After I was done, I stood up and washed my face. I rinsed my mouth out and started to feel better just doing that. I looked over at the tub and thought about climbing in and making all of me feel better. I stripped my nightgown off and climbed into the shower. The water was set as lukewarm, trying to break the fever. I washed my hair and already felt better. I was soaping up my big belly when I heard Asher in my head.

Woman, are you trying to kill me?

I let out a laugh and forgot that the link was open. He could see my mind and everything that I was doing. I gave a wicked grin and started to rub my sore breast with soap bubbles.

Yes, you are trying to kill me. I came back to tell you that you are in the start of labor, and here you are giving me all these sexual images. I need to get you back now! I cannot take this much longer.

Then come and get me, Asher.

I chuckled when I heard him let out a groan.

Woman, you will be the death of me. Now I need you to listen to me about your labor, so come on out of that shower and put clothes on. I cannot focus while you are all soapy.

I laughed and washed my body clean, grabbing a towel afterward. I put my clothes on and sat on the side of the bed.

Okay, I am ready.

This is the first part of labor. It is going to be harder on you because I am not with you. You are still far apart. So we have a long way to go. I hope I am with you before they come. I am sorry that I am not there. I feel like a horrible mate.

Now you listen to me, Asher! You are my rock. You will be a great father, and you are an awesome mate.

How can I be a good mate when you are there and I am here? This is not being a good mate.

Speaking of which, where are you now?

We are halfway to you. Mike became the beta after Eric pulled this stunt. He is driving right now, and I am in the back seat talking to you.

I am so sorry you lost your best friend and beta because of me.

No, I lost a fake friend because he is a puppet to his parents. Has nothing to do with you. This was their plan all along, and they would have taken whoever it was. It makes me wonder if he is the reason why my first mate is gone.

You never did tell me what happened to her.

She was pregnant like you. She went for a walk in the woods and never came back. I tried and tried to contact her through the link, but it was just dead. Around the time that she gave birth, I felt the mate bond die. I felt the pup bond die. I do not know what happened to her to this day. It took me months on top of years to get over it. I broke. Eric was the one that picked me back up. I never did find out what happened to her.

You do not say her name.

It hurts to say it, but her name is Violet.

Well, not to make fun of it, but you have a thing for flowers.

What do you mean?

Her name was Violet. Mine is Rose, my last name.

Hey, I did not even think of that. I guess I do.

Someone is coming. Listen in.

My door slammed open, and in walked the king.

"Hello, King Steven. How are you tonight?"

He stood there looking at me, breathing hard.

"I have been trying to sleep, but you are keeping me awake."

I looked at him with a confused look on my face. How was I keeping him up?

"I have heard you sick. That must mean that you have started to go into labor. Without your mate with you, that is what will happen. If you get to the point that it will kill you, we will open you up and take that pup out of you."

No way in hell will that happen. We are coming faster, hang on.

"Sir, I am a strong woman. It will not come to that. Thank you for checking on me."

He walked over to me and grabbed me up by my arms. The grip was so tight that I knew he would leave marks on me. I was not going to show that I felt the pain.

"Keep your mouth shut. You might be pretty, but your mouth is horrible."

Then he threw me on the bed. He turned around and walked out of the room. I took a deep breath and pulled myself up against the wall.

We are almost there. Hang on, Willow.

Okay.

CHAPTER

As the day went on, my labor started to move faster. I tried to get a hold of Asher, but he was not there. My heart broke for a little bit, then I remembered he was coming for me. I was lying in bed breathing harder and watching my clock. I was now at twenty minutes apart. The pain was unreal. I thought for sure my pup was an alien trying to tear their way out of me. I had not had anything to eat all day and only took sips of water. I changed out of the nightgown and put on an oversized shirt and little-boy shorts. I wanted to feel cool, but it was not helping. I had the windows opened and a fan in one of them, hoping and praying that it would make me feel better. Nothing was making me feel better. I needed Asher. That was the only thing that would make me feel better. Oh, and getting this pup out of me. My stomach started to ease up, so I got up from the bed, thinking that walking around the room would help me. I had gone around the room four times when I heard a gunshot.

I looked around the room for a hiding spot when I saw a crack in the wall. I walked over to it and felt around it. The wall opened somehow. I started to feel everything and move things around trying to find the trigger. I pulled on a book that was on top of the fireplace, and the wall folded back. I looked inside the wall, and there was a small room. It had a love seat in it and a little lamp. I walked over to it and turned on the light. This looked like a good place to hide, and maybe then I would live through this. I walked back over to the room and grabbed my water and pillow. I walked back into the room and pushed the button, and the door closed.

I hope I can breathe in here.

I lay back on the love seat with my pillow behind me checking the time. Now I was fifteen minutes apart. This was moving too fast for me. As I was sitting there, I was also looking around the small room. Nothing much to look at, but there was a frame on the wall. Not knowing what it was or why it was just there, I got up and walked over to it. I saw some buttons on the side in the wall in a line. I pushed the top button, and nothing happened. I pushed the second button, and the wall opened. Behind it was a TV screen. Now the frame had something in it. I pushed the top button again, and the TV came on. I could see all around the house. They had cameras set up everywhere.

I pushed the third button, and the AC kicked on. Now this is what I really needed. There was one more button. I reached down and pushed it, and the TV changed to the outside. There were six different little camera views. I sat back down and watched what was going on.

I saw several wolves coming out of the woods. I was several wolves coming out of the house. I prayed for Asher and all his wolves that were getting ready to fight for me. The front line of Asher's wolves came into a full run, jumping on the first line of wolves. There were biting and ripping of fur and skin. I saw wolves falling to the ground that were a part of my pack. My heart was breaking as I watched them die. The other wolves let their guard up and were jumping around howling at the sky. I saw one wolf twitch. I thought they turn human when they die, but all of these wolves were still wolves. I looked at the twitching wolf to see what was going on. As one of the wolves walked past him, the wolf reached out and bit his leg. It looked like it was painful because the wolf was howling at the sky. The wolf jumped up from the ground and jumped on top of him, ripping his neck out. I turned my head away so I did not see the blood. When I looked back, the wolf had turned back into a human, and all the other wolves were up and fighting again.

I looked out to the trees and saw more wolves out watching. It was easy to see them for me because their eyes were glowing in the camera. I was watching only one now. He was sitting by a tree looking up at the camera.

Willow, I am coming for you. Just breathe, and I will be there soon.

Asher! I am in a small panic room. I found it in my room. When you get to the room that has a bed pushed to the wall and the blankets are all over the ground, with dark-blue walls, I need to you to tell me you are here. No one can come in because I have locked it from the inside.

You are one of kind, Willow. I am coming.

I can see you.

How?

There is a secret system in here. You are sitting next to a tree looking at the camera.

I love you, Willow.

I love you too, Asher.

The link was broken, and he smiled at the camera. I love it when a wolf smiles. It is just the cutest thing. But I would never tell him that he was cute. I watched as Asher got up and backed up to the woods. I looked down at my watch to see that I was now ten minutes apart. Maybe I should have told him that. My pain had picked up, but not much I could do about that now. I moved from lying down to sitting up, anything to make it feel a little better. I was walking around the small room when I heard a pound on the wall. I stopped and looked over at the door. I walked over to it and saw more buttons on it. I thought hard before I pushed the top button. The top of the door opened to a window. I was able to see out, but I did not think they could see in. I watched as Patrick walked around the room throwing all the stuff around. I watched him walk into the bathroom and come back out slamming the door shut. I loved watching him be confused. After what he did to me, I hoped they killed him. I pushed the second button, and a speaker turned on.

"I cannot find her anywhere. Well, what do you want me to do? No, I cannot pull her out of thin air. It is like she just disappeared. I have looked under everything. Oh, for the love of God, she is not in this room, Eric!"

Well, Eric was looking for me now. I was so glad that I found this room. Patrick slammed his phone into the wall and sat on the floor, leaning on the wall. I was so confused as to what he was doing when Eric came running into the room.

"Where the hell is she, Patrick!" Eric yelled at him.

Patrick just sat there and shrugged his shoulders. Next thing I knew, there was a gunshot, and Patrick fell down the wall, laying on the floor. Eric shot him between the eyes. There was no coming back from that one. Eric looked around the room, and his eyes landed on the door I was standing behind. He walked over to it and pressed his face to it.

"I know you are in there, Willow. I am guessing that you can hear me also. I will win and get that pup. Get the hell out here and face what is coming."

I reached down and pushed the last button.

"I will never come out of there. You will never have my pup. Die first."

Eric yelled and slammed his hands on the door. My contractions picked that point to start coming on strong and fast.

Asher, can you hear me?

Yes. Make it fast please.

I am three minutes apart, and Eric is outside the door trying to get it. He is yelling and slamming his body into the door. Please hurry.

On my way. Hold on tight.

I looked at Eric one more time and pushed the buttons to turn off the sound of him and the window. I walked over to the love seat and sat down. Trying to find some way to sit comfortably was so out of the question right now. I moved the pillow up the arm of the seat and leaned back on it. While I was sitting there, I saw another button on the wall by my head. Next to it was a post note.

Do not push this button until your mate says you are safe to. Be careful.

Well that was odd. I was breathing hard and fast when I remembered the buttons to the TV. I got up and made my way over to it and pressed the button for the inside of the house. I saw four wolves inside the house tearing everyone in their way apart.

I watched the larger wolf just for a few seconds before the pup made it known that it was time. I walked back over to the love seat praying Asher made it on time. I pulled my boy shorts off and climbed back into leaning on the armrest. I turned my head to find the big wolf. I watched as it ripped three other wolves apart in a blink of an eye. He really was in a hurry. I looked to the screen that was of my room door. I watched as the wolf broke the door down in one shot. I did not see anything else after that since there was no camera in my room. Well, that I knew of. I waited for a little bit, not knowing what was going on. Then the link was opened.

Eric, you tell me now! What happened to Violet?

I will never tell you. I am the only one that knows, and if I do not tell you, you will keep me alive.

I felt something in my back stab me, and it freaked me out. I reached back to rub it, and I hit something. I moved forward and grabbed whatever it was. There was a book in my hand. It was the color violet. I opened the book and read the first page.

Asher, if you read this, I am dead, and your new mate has been taken. This is everything that has happened to me since you last saw me. Asher's mate, tell him you have this so he can kill Eric.

I looked up so fast my head felt like I snapped it off.

Asher, you can kill him. I have a book that Violet wrote that will tell you everything.

How can I trust that?

Because you love me and your pup.

Okay.

It was quiet for a little bit in my head, and I was getting the feeling that I needed to push. I looked up at the TV again to see that there was a pile of humans on the ground and Mike standing there with gasoline. He started to dump it on them. Then he lit it on fire and looked up at the camera, smiled at me, and gave me a thumbs up.

Willow, you can let me in now. Eric is dead.

I pushed the button, and the door slid open. Asher came running to me, falling to his knees.

"I am so sorry for everything that has happened. I hope you will be able to forgive me."

"I will only forgive you if you help me bring your pup into this world. It is time."

I watched him get up and walk away. My heart was breaking with every step he took. He turned to look at me and smiled at me, then reached up and pushed the close button. He walked back over to me and sat on the other side of the seat.

"Let us bring our pup into this world together. Just you and me."

I smiled at him and braced myself for the fight of my life.

Willow looked up at Asher and let out a weak smile. She was ready to get this pup out of her and was going to do everything in her power to make it through. She had sweat dripping from her forehead while Asher was looking around for anything he could use to help her. He found a small box under the table. He pulled it out and saw a note on the top of it.

Asher, use this to help your mate bring your pup into the world.

Asher looked up to Willow, raising his eyebrow. "How did this person know that we would be in here like this? It is kind of freaking me out."

Willow smiled at him and nodded her head.

"Yeah, it has been freaking me out since I got into this room."

Asher nodded his head and opened the box to look inside of it. He found washcloths and scissors. He pulled out the washcloth and smelled it. Not smelling anything but cleanness, he used it to wipe Willow's head.

"Thanks."

"Willow, I need to look and see if the pup's head is coming out. Do you think you can let me do that?"

Willow nodded at Asher as she lay back and displayed herself to him.

"Okay, I can see a little part of his hair. I am going to need you to push."

Holding herself up by her knees, she pushed with all her might. She let out a scream.

"Asher, I need you up here to stop the pain. How are we to do this when you cannot be in both spots?" Willow cried at him.

Asher was looking around trying to figure out what to do. Both of their heads snapped to the wall as another door opened. In walked the one person that Asher thought he would never see again.

"Violet?" came his whisper.

Willow looked over at Asher and saw love, worry, and confusion as he looked at his dead mate—well, whom he thought was dead. "What is going on?"

"I will explain everything after Willow is safe. Go up to her head and help your mate bring your pup into this world. I will help down here if that is okay with you, Willow?"

Willow nodded her head fast as she let out another scream. Both parts got into place—Asher up by her head and picking her up so she could lean on him and Violet down to help deliver the pup. After many screams and pushes later, the pup was out of Willow. Violet placed the pup down on the love seat on a towel and began to clean their nose and mouth out.

She then held up the scissors to Asher. "Would you like to cut the cord to your new son?"

Asher looked at her with wide eyes. "I have a son?"

You could see the smile grow on his face. He grabbed the scissors from her and cut where she told him to. After he was wrapped up in a towel, she went to hand him to Willow, but Asher reached for the pup with a smile on his face.

"Hello, little guy. I am your dad." He smiled down at the pup.

He had black hair like midnight and bright-blue eyes. Asher was so busy talking to the pup that he did not see what was going on beside him.

"Willow, I need you to push the last part out. Do you think you can do that? You are losing so much blood that we have to try to stop it."

Willow gave a weak nod and pushed yet again. She fell back on the love seat with sweat pouring off her. Willow knew her life was slipping away. She would not be able to see her pup because Asher, for some reason, would not let her see him. Her heart was breaking slowly.

"Willow, I am going to have to save you. I am sorry for what I am about to do."

Willow looked at her with tears in her eyes. All she wanted was her baby. She felt a sharp pain in her skin by her leg and looked down to see what was going on. She saw Violet had cut her open. Willow closed her eyes and held in the scream so she would not scare the pup. She was slipping into the darkness and knew, if she let it come, she would never get back out. Slowly she opened her eyes and saw that Asher no longer had the pup in his hands. He had his hands on Violet's hands.

"Why did you leave me?"

"Asher, I am trying to save your mate."

"You are my mate."

"No, I am not. Willow is your mate."

"Willow who?"

"What are you talking about, Asher? Willow, the lady lying on this love seat dying from bringing your pup into this world."

Willow could hear that Violet was getting upset. There was nothing she could do but just lie there and wait. Violet pushed Asher to the side and once again got to work on her.

"Willow, I need you to stay awake. Talk to me about something. Anything. Please."

"I no longer know what is going on. I have not seen my pup and have no idea why Asher is doing this. I do not know why he is pushing me away yet again or why he will not even look at me. All he sees is the pup and you. I feel like I do not matter anymore. Please just let me die. No one needs me anymore. I am not important to anyone."

I felt a tear run down my cheek as I looked up at Violet. I saw tears in her eyes also. I know this was hard for her, trying to save the mate of her true mate.

"Willow, you listen to me. Asher is no longer my mate. I took steps for him to lose the mate bond and for him to think I was dead. I do not know what is going on with him right now. But I will explain it all to you when you are better. Now let me heal you."

Willow's eyes closed again, and she fell into a sleep as Violet worked on saving her life. After she cut her open, she was able to find the bleeding vein and sewed it closed. She then stitched her back together. It was not the most perfect save, but it was what she could do with what she had. When she was done, she looked up at Asher.

"You are a stupid man! How could you sit there talking to me like that while I was trying to save your mate? You really are a stupid man. What the hell happened?"

Asher looked at her like she had grown two heads. What was she talking about?

"I do not know what you are talking about. You gave birth to our pup. This is our pup. I do not know a Willow. I do not know what is going on with you."

Violet stood up and pulled a bed into the room and went over to Willow and picked her up and laid her down on it. She then attached a little baby crib next to the bed and went to the pup and picked him up. She placed the pup next to Willow and pulled her top to the side so she could get to her breast.

"Sorry, Willow, but I am going to touch you now. I need to feed your pup and give you two skin to skin."

Asher jumped up to stop her from doing it.

"Sit your ass down on that couch, and do not move!" she yelled at him.

He slowly sat back down. Violet turned back to Willow and moved both Willow and the pup around to get him to latch onto her and drink. She smiled down at them for a couple of minutes before turning back to Asher.

"We have a lot to talk about. But first, I need to figure out what is wrong with you. I will be right back."

Violet turned and walked out of the door, closing it behind her. She walked to the wall and looked through the one-way mirror hoping Asher would know who Willow was after she left the room. And sure enough, he did. He jumped up and ran to her side, pushing her hair from her eyes. He smiled down at her and the pup. That put a smile on Violet's face. She sat down at her desk and pulled out a book, looking to see what was going on and what she could do to fix it.

Willow slowly opened her eyes and looked around the room. Her pup was lying next to her, feeding off her. She looked for Asher but could not find him anywhere. What had happened to him? She willed her body to get up and to look around. As soon as her pup was done, she climbed out of the bed and walked to the door that was locked from the inside. She pushed the first button, and the window opened to her. She looked out and saw nothing. She closed the window and started to look around again. She saw some buttons to the left of the love seat. She walked over to it and pushed the top button. The wall opened to another window. She pushed the love seat out of the way and looked through it. She could hardly make it out as the room was so dark, so she walked over and shut the lights off. Walking back over, she made sure that her pup was okay before going back to the window. She got to it, and all her breath was knocked out of her. There standing in the room was Asher and Violet kissing. Her mind turned blank as she watched her mate cheat on her.

She pushed the second button to turn on the sound. She watched as Violet pushed him away.

"Asher, would you please stop and listen to me!"

Asher stopped what he was doing and sat down like a robot.

"I have a spell on me that makes all males forget about their mates and try to get with me. You must fight it before Willow sees and leaves you! I would never hurt her. You have to fight it and remember your mate."

She took a step back and picked up a big book. Then she started to say words that Willow could not make out. She watched Asher as his eyes turned from a deep red to his blue eyes. Asher shook his head as if coming out of a fog.

"Where am I? Violet, what is going on? Where is Willow and my pup?"

Violet looked like she could fight the world with the smile on her face.

"Willow and your pup are in the next room." Then she turned and smiled at the window like she knew that Willow was there. "Let me explain it all to you, okay?"

Asher nodded his head and waited for what she had to say.

"I went for a run when the king and queen's guard caught up with me. They told me that you were with them waiting on me to get there. So I went with them, thinking I would run into you at their house. I went willing, Asher. But only because they said you were waiting with them for me. I was kept in the same room as Willow for two months before I started to plan and plot. I was able to talk one of the guards to help me. He would sneak stuff to me as we changed the closet into the room Willow is in now. He helped me set it all up. So that way, when I had the pup, I could hide in that room. He was going to bring me food while I hid and keep me safe. When we got done with that room, we started on this room. This would be my room after the pup was born, and we both would be safe. I tried to mind-link you several times. But it never worked, and we could not figure out was wrong.

"After we got the rooms done, he left and did not come back for several weeks. When he did come back, he had a witch with him. He told me she was going to put a spell on me so, that way, I could be able to mind-link you. I agreed with it, and so the spell was placed. I did not know he lied to me. I had a horrible labor, and the pup died before I could get him out. The guard came back to the room, and I let him in, falling into his arms crying while our dead pup was lying on the love seat. He told me how sorry he was, that he could bring the witch back to make me forget it ever happened. I was okay with that so I did not feel the pain.

"Again, it was a couple of days before they showed back up. I was in my room where Willow is, still holding my son. The witch came in and removed him from my arms and placed him in a basket. Told me she could bury him for me. I asked her to help me get free, and she told me that she could not do that, for the king and queen would kill her. Then she went on with her spell. I felt funny. I had no clue what was happening. I felt like my head was going to blow up, and I passed out. When I woke up, I was in a different room, and that guard was standing over me. He told me that he was going to love me forever and give me the pup that I had always wanted. I fought him as much as I could, but in the end, he won. He raped me several times before I fell pregnant with his pup. I was kept in the room for the full pregnancy, then when I had the pup, she was taken from me.

"When the witch came back, she thanked me for the pup she could not have. She then took me back to my room that I built. She told me about Willow and that the queen was going to do everything in her power to get her here. So I then started to make this room for Willow. At the time, I did not know who she was or what was going to happen. I wanted to be there for her even if I could not help her to get her out. I would check every now and then to see if they got her. And then I saw her. She was so pretty. Her belly was big at the time she got here, so I knew it would not be long before she gave birth. I tried to mind-link you to let you know where she was so she did not get hurt like I did. But again, I could not.

"So I got ready to help her have her pup. If she had not found the room, I would have gone out and gotten her. I watched her fight off every attack that came her way. I was so proud that you found a fighter as a new mate. I loved her even though I had not met her. I knew she was the right one for you. There was one night when she was sleeping that I went into her room. I washed her forehead from the sweat on her brow and just talked to the pup, telling him about his dad and what a great man he was. I had no clue how you two were in the relationship, but I wanted the little guy to know about his dad. I saw her get up and run to the bathroom one night, sick, and knew it was time for her to go into labor. What surprised me the most was, when she was sitting on her bed with her eyes closed, like she was talking to someone. When she got up and started to walk around the room, I knew she would find this room, so I moved to the back room. And as you know the rest, I will save you from it."

"How did you eat?"

"Several guards knew about me. They would place food by the door, and I would open it and get it. I was well taken care of by them. Never would they see me because of the spell."

"How did you find out about the spell?"

"The witch came to me after about a year and told me about it. Came to find out the guard that helped me was her mate. They made a pact with each other to help me just so I could give them the pup they could not have. She placed the spell on me because her mate fell in love with me and wanted nothing to do with her. So she placed this spell on me. When a male look into my eyes, the spell is set. I have not been able to get rid of it yet." She smiled at him and then smiled at the wall.

Willow let out a breath she did not know she was holding in.

"Willow told me that she had a new pair of earrings in, that she did not know where they came from or how she got them. But a voice in her head told her to take them out. She did, and she could mind-link me then, that the earrings were holding it back. You do not have earrings, but is there something, maybe on your body, that you do not know where it came from?"

Violet thought for a moment before she pulled off her shoe and sock, looking down at the toe ring. She pulled it off and held it up, looking at it.

"This is not the one you got me. It looks just like it, but when you are looking inside of it, there is no 'V+A' inside of it."

Violet handed it over to Asher. He looked at it when he heard a voice in his head.

Asher, can you hear me?

Yeah, I can.

Violet broke down in tears. "All this time, and it was that damn ring. But now that that is all over, we move on."

"What are we going to do? You are still my mate," Asher asked her.

"Do you still feel the mate bond with me? Not the spell?"

Willow held her breath waiting to see what he said. Would she lose another mate now? Would her and her pup be kicked out?

"I do not know what the pull is. I do not know if it is the mate bond or the spell. I know I love Willow, but I have loved you longer then her. You are my true mate. She is my picked mate."

"So you are saying you would throw it all away? Your mate bond with Willow? Your pup? You would give it all up to be with me?"

"Why do I have to give it all up? Why cannot I have both of you?"

Willow moved away from the window with tears in her eyes. She looked at her pup in the crib sleeping. She walked over to the other door and looked out. There was no one there, so she walked back to her pup and picked him up.

"Guess it is just you and me, bud. I will give you the world, I promise. Might take me a little bit, but I will give you the world."

With that, Willow walked out of the room and into the hall. She looked both ways before she went down the hall looking for a way out. As she came to a door, she could hear stuff moving behind it. She tried to be as quiet as possible, but it was not quiet enough. The door swung open, and Mike walked out.

"Willow, thank gosh! Where is Asher?"

"Hello, Mike, he is in a hidden room with Violet, his old mate."

Mike looked like he had seen ghost when I said that.

"What are you going to do?"

"Asher said he wanted the both of us. I am not one to share, so I am going to give him his mate. I am going to leave and not be seen again."

"Are you sure? I do not want you to leave, Willow. You are the best Luna we have ever had."

"Mike, thank you, but I have to go. I will not come between them. If Asher wants her, then I will step away."

Mike pulled me into the room. I looked around and saw a desk and bookshelves and two chairs and a couch. This had to have been the king's office.

"If you are sure about this and you are going to leave, then let me help you."

I guess he saw the fear on my face because he said, "I will not tell Asher where you go. If he picked Violet, then I will get you, my Luna, and her pup, my little alpha to safety."

I nodded my head at him and sat down with him while we figured out where I was going.

After about an hour, we figured out where I was going and what I needed to get there. Mike had been on the phone getting it all figured out. He was great. After all was said and done, I was going to an island off the coast of Puerto Rico. There was a small town on the island full of humans. I could do this. The plane would leave in an hour. Mike stood up and told me to follow him. I moved behind him, carrying my little one. I still needed to name him. Mike took me to a car and told me to get the little one in the car seat in it. I placed him in and then climbed in after. Mike looked at me and smiled before he started the car. Soon we were driving down the long drive. Mike stopped at the guard gate. Someone investigated the car and smiled at Mike.

"Mike, where are you going with the Luna and the pup?"

"Payton, I am taking them shopping. We have nothing for the pup here."

"Does the alpha know you are taking them out?"

"Come on, man. I am not that stupid. Of course, he knows. He is busy with other stuff to be the one to take them. Now let me out."

The guard looked at me one more time before he let us out. Mike let out a breath and started to drive away. It took about two hours to get to the airport.

"I am sorry, Willow. I am sorry that Asher did this to you. No one should go through as much as you have. I am sorry that your pup will grow up without his dad. I am just so sorry. I have always liked you as my Luna and as my friend."

Willow looked up at him and saw tears in his eyes. "Hey, Mike, do you want to come with me?"

"Are you for real? I am the beta of this pack now. What will Asher do when he finds out?"

"If Asher finds out, then just tell him you went with me to protect me."

Mike raised an eyebrow and thought for a minute. Then he called the airline to see if there was another ticket. When he got the word that there was, he bought it on the spot and agreed to go with me. I got out of the car and picked up my pup. I still had to name him. Mike walked to back of the car and pulled out a backpack and a big bag. I looked at him, and he just smiled at me. He then grabbed another bag out of the trunk and handed it to me. When he saw my confused face, he told me it had baby stuff in it. I placed it on my shoulder, and together we walked to the airport. Time to find a new life.

CHAPTER

30

After a little bit, we made it to the plane. I found my seat and sat down. The man next to me looked at me with fear in his eyes when he saw the pup. Mike walked up to me and saw the face of the man.

"Hey, man, my seat is way over there. If you want to, you can have my seat. That would help me anyways since that is my wife and kid."

The man looked at the baby one more time and then nodded his head and got up. They changed seats, and Mike sat down by me. We got ready for the plane to take off. After we were in the air, the pup fell asleep, and Mike and I just sat there. I got tired of the silence, so I broke it.

"So I need to name little man. You go any ideas on what it should be?"

Mike looked at me for a little bit before he opened his mouth.

"You want me to help you name him? He is not even mine. Why would you want my help?"

I smiled up at Mike and thought for a second before I opened my mouth.

"You and I are in this together now that you have left the pack. You will be a part of my life and his life. I thought it would be fun if you helped me name him. But if that is too much, I understand."

"No, no, not at all. I just could not believe that you wanted my help." He looked down at the pup asleep on my lap and smiled at him. "I feel a pull to this guy. I could because he was to be the next alpha of my pack. When I walked away from the pack, the pull should have been broken. However, the pull has gotten stronger to both of you. I have no clue what this pull is, but I will be with you guys every step of the way. And I think Bryan Matthew is a good strong name. It is what I had picked out if I ever had a pup."

I looked up and saw the sadness in his eyes. "Mike, what happened to your mate? The sadness in your eyes gives you away."

Mike let out a deep breath. He looked out the window for a little bit before he turned back to me, ready to talk. "Is the name what you want?"

I nodded at him, smiling big. "Bryan Matthew Rose."

Mike smiled at me. "I like that. Now about my mate. This trip is long, but the story is not." He let out a little laugh, then turned back to the window. "My mate and I were best friends since diapers. Her name was Scarlet. We grew up together and did everything together. I was a year older, so when I turned sixteen and found out she was my mate, I was over the moon. I wanted to tell her on the spot, but she said one thing that changed my mind. 'I hope I am Asher's mate. To be Luna of the pack and carry his pups would be a dream come true.'

"That is when I made up my mind to make her fall in love with me in a year. I pulled out all the stops with dates and outings. I kept away from Asher for the year, trying to get him out of her mind. But nothing helped. The day before her sixteenth birthday, she told me that she was going to run into his arms the second she knows that he is her mate. I looked at her with sad eyes, but she did not notice. I finally had enough and started to yell at her, asking what was wrong with me. Why could she not love me the way I loved her? She laughed at me and told me it would be like kissing her brother, that she did not want anything to do with me but as a best friend. My heart broke, and I just walked away.

"She yelled my name several times, but I just kept walking. I did not know where I was going, but I ended up at a cliff. I sat down and looked up at the sky with all the stars and just rested there. I heard a scream and turned around. There was Scarlet yelling at me not to jump, that she was not worth taking my own life. I know I looked at her like she grew two heads. Why would I jump over a girl? That is simply crazy. When I told her, I was just looking at the stars and to go back to her party. She told me she could not go without me. I told her that I would not watch her run to Asher. She turned and walked off, leaving me there.

"After a little while, I changed into my wolf and just started to walk around. I found a creek about a mile away from the cliff and drank some water. My wolf was going crazy to get to his mate. I had to hold him back. She did not want us. Why fight something I would never win? But she found me sitting there by the creek. She jumped at me and wrapped her arms around my neck. I sat as still as I could. I did not think she knew it was me. She started to talk to me and tell me all about herself which made me know she did not know it was me. After about an hour like this, she finally asked me to change back. I knew this was not going to go well, so I changed in front of her and placed my hands down below so she did not see it. She started to yell at me for lying to her. She demanded to know where her true mate was. I moved to her, so the sparks would move all over her. She was crying and jumped up and ran away.

"It was almost a month before I saw her again. She had changed a lot and was just staring at me. I walked over to her, and we talked. I found out that she had sex with some stranger and got pregnant from it. I told her I would still be her mate and father to the kid. She agreed, and I marked her. It hurt like hell because we both did not love each other. I took care of her while she was pregnant, but she did not care. When she went into labor, she was ripped apart with pain. There was nothing I could do since I was not the father of the pup. She died trying to bring the pup into the world. The pup lived. The father came and got him after the birth. Her family knew what had happened and contacted the man. I was once again without a mate and pup. I never looked for a second-chance mate. I did not want to go through that again." Mike hung his head down and took a deep breath.

"You are the first one I have said all that to."

I reached out and held his hand, smiling up at him.

"Thank you for telling me. I will tell no one. Together, we will be okay."

He agreed, and we sat quiet for the rest of the plane ride watching the little man sleep.

When we landed, Mike got a car to take us to the rental place. When we got there, Mike helped us out of the car and got all our stuff. We walked into the building, and there stood an older-looking woman.

"Hello, may I help you?"

Mike spoke up first. "Hello to you too. I am looking for VI."

"VI? I know no one by that name."

"That is a bummer. She was my step-sister-in-law."

I looked at Mike weird. What the heck was he talking about?

"She would be sad that she would miss her stepmom's niece today."

Then they shook hands in a weird way—fist bump, then slaps to the right, then to the left with their hands flying around after it. My eyes were wide when they were done doing all of this.

"Hello, Mike and Willow. We are glad to have you on the island."

"Okay, what the heck was all of that?" I almost yelled.

Mike turned and smiled at me.

"Willow, this is VI. She has been getting everything set up for us. But we made sure that no one could find us by setting up all of that. It is a code that only VI and I knew. She will help keep us safe."

I nodded my head. I trust Mike. So we were taken into the back room and out the back door. There was an SUV waiting for us with tinted windows. Mike helped me in and then handed me Bryan. He closed the door and climbed in next to me. VI got in the front and started the SUV.

She showed us where the stores are at. She showed us where the bank was at. She showed us where the town hall was. She then drove to the other side of the island. There was nothing but thick palm trees everywhere. She turned down a road between two trees and took off fast. I held onto Bryan, afraid of her driving. We pulled up in front of the most beautiful house I had ever seen.

"Everything is here and ready for you guys. The keys to everything is on the table. I have loaded the house with everything you asked for. I hope you love living here. When you need supplies, just ask, and I will come running. Your bank information is also on the table. Bye." And then she was gone.

I looked over at Mike, and he was laughing.

"What the heck was that, Mike?"

"That, Willow, was a lady that I called up and found. She works in the rental office, and she said she would take care of everything for me. She knows we ran away and do not want to be found. She charged me, and that was not nice, but I also understand you got to make a living."

"Speaking of living, what are we going to do for money, and how did you afford all of this?" I waved my hand in front of the house and beach that was at the back of it.

"Would you believe that I had all this money?"

I shook my head no.

"Okay, fine. I may have stolen money and added it to what I already had."

"Mike! They will look for us now 'cause of the money."

"No, we are in the clear. I took it from somewhere no one will find. We will be good."

I smiled up at Mike and then looked at the house. It was not too big but not too small either. It was blue in color, so it was kind of blended in with the ocean. There was a deck that looked like it wrapped around it. We walked up the stairs and inside. It was pretty and homey feeling. The living room was to the right, and the kitchen was to the left. There were floor-to-ceiling windows. The stairs were in front of me, so I went up. Why not? I came to the first door and opened it up. It had a guy feel to it and was huge. I walked back up and open the door next to it. It was a nursery. There were little wolves running all over the wall. The theme of werewolves was cute. I walked over and placed Bryan into the crib and walked back out. I moved to the next door which was on the other side of the hall across from Bryan.

I opened the door; and it had a nice, girly, warm feeling to it. I looked around, and there was a big, soft-looking bed. There was a vanity to the side under the windows and a dresser on the other wall. I saw two doors and opened the first one. It was a walk-in closet, big enough for another room. Crazy. It was already filled with women clothes. I walked out and closed the door. I walked to the next one and opened it. The bathroom was good sized. Had his-and-her sinks, big shower, toilet across the room, and a big claw tub. I could not wait to give it a try.

"I see you found your room."

I jumped when I heard Mike's voice.

"Sorry." I heard him say with a chuckle coming out.

"Funny."

We went back downstairs and talked over the rules of living together. We handed out keys to the house and cars. We went over the bank and the cards for that, plus the rules. By the time we were done, I was done. I just wanted to go to bed. But Bryan woke up then. I walked to his room and took care of him. Since he was only a week old, he slept a lot, giving time to heal my body. After I was done with him, I walked over to my room ready for a bath. I sat on the edge of the bed to pull my shoes off. Well that did not work as I fell back and fell into a deep, deep sleep.

CHAPTER

Dream.

I was walking in a green field. There were wildflowers here and there. I laid my hand out so that, as I walked, it brushed the top to the grass. I could hear something in the wind but could not make out what it was. I was walking all around not being able to find a way out. I tried to call out, but my voice seemed to be stuck in my throat.

What is going on?

I turned around when I heard movement in the grass, but my eyes landed on nothing. I turned back around and came face-to-face with Asher. I jumped back and let out a shaky breath.

"Hello, Willow. Did you think I could not find you? Did you think you could take my child and hide from me?"

I looked at him with wide eyes and tried to talk yet again, but the same thing happened. My voice was cut off in my throat.

"Yes, you cannot talk. I want you to listen to me and listen well. You are my mate. That is my pup. Wherever you are, you need to come back. You are nowhere you should be. I have a lot to explain to you and want you to sit down here with me and listen. Can you do that?"

I nodded my head and looked down. Next to me was a blue blanket. I slipped off my shoes and pulled my sundress just a little and sat down. I was playing with my fingers by the time he sat down. He let out a deep breath before he turned to me and talked.

"That day, that horrible day, I was under a spell. Violet is a witch now. She cast a spell on me to get me to say all those horrible things. She knew you were listening, and she wanted to break you. I am so sorry that she was able to do that. I do not want her. I wanted to know what happened to her. That is all I wanted to know. I will never forgive myself for what I did to you. I was able to get out because a guard showed up to feed her and she opened the door up. I jumped her and knocked her out. I ran with everything I had. When I made it to the pack border, the spell broke on me. I came back to the pack house praying that you came back here with Mike. But when I got back, you both were gone. I have been looking for you both since I got free a day ago. Willow, no words can ever make this better. I do love you, and I do miss you already. What have you named our son?"

"Bryan Matthew Rose." I hung my head. "I want to forgive you. I want to believe that this is all true. I want to run back into your arms. But how do I know this is not a lie? That my mind is just making it all up?"

What was I meant to do? This was just a dream, right? I looked up at Asher, and he reached over and touched me. I felt the tingles spread all over my body. This dream was messed up.

"Willow, this is not a dream. This is a dream-walk. I have finally found you. I have been looking everywhere to find you. But I guess you had not gone to bed yet. I could feel the mate bond pulling me to you. I could feel your want for me. I am sorry, Willow. Nothing I say or do will make it better, but I will fight with all I got to get you both back. I must go now. Our son is about to wake up. Please take good care of both of you guys. I love you both."

I looked up, and he was gone. I was all alone in the field. I hung my head and let out silent tears. What was I going to do? Do I believe him, or do I let it all go? I had no idea what to do about it.

"You forgive him, and you move on with your mate," came a woman's voice next to me, making me jump out of my skin.

My head snapped over to the voice and saw the most beautiful woman sitting next to me.

"Hello, Willow, I am Sky. I am the Moon Goddess of the were-wolves. I have come to have a chat with you. Is that okay?"

I nodded my head and turned to face her.

"You, my child, have been through a lot in your short little life. I am sorry you have gone through so much. I know you do not really

BIRTH OF THE CHOSEN ONE

know who I am as you are a shape-shifter, but you are going to be raising a mighty alpha. I am here to help you on your way. There are a few things I can do for you. First, I can break the mate bond with Asher. He did not know what he was saying because he was under a spell. He came to me in tears over it and asked to dream-walk, and I allowed it. That way, he could tell you everything himself. He has told you the truth as I have watched over it all. I will break the mate bond with him if asked. Second, I can give you a new mate, like Mike. He has taken your child himself to be the dad of him. I can make you two mates. Third, I can wipe your memory of everything that has happened in your life. I can give you a new start with Mike. Your son is going to grow up to be a strong and mighty alpha. If you choose this path, then you will lose your son at some point in his life. He will never forgive you for taking his dad away. The last thing I can give you is the chance to be with Asher again, to love him and be his mate, to raise your son with his father. You have two weeks to make up your mind as to what you want. I will see you again then." And then she was gone.

CHAPTER

33

I woke up covered in sweat. What the heck was that? I heard Bryan crying across the room from me. I got up and walked over to him. Just looking down at him made my heart soar. I picked him up and carried him back to my bed, changed him, and fed him. While I was feeding him, I thought I would talk to him.

"So, little guy, what do you say? Do we go back to your dad and forgive him, or do we stay here with Uncle Mike?" I just looked at him, waiting for him to give me a look so I knew which way to go.

Go back to dad, came a voice inside my head, making me jump.

"What the heck was that?" I asked, looking all around.

I did not know that voice. I have never heard it before.

Momma, I want to go back to Dad. This is me, Bryan, talking in your head. Look at my eyes, and you will see that I am talking to you.

I looked down at him, and I could see it in his eyes. He was telling the truth. My pup was talking to me, and he was only a week old. Then I remembered what the Moon Goddess said to me. He would be mighty and strong. Now I really believed what she said.

"You want to go home, but how do I forgive him for everything?" I asked, looking down at Bryan.

It is easy, Momma. He was under a spell. He did not know what he was doing.

I just looked at him with wide eyes. This was weird.

I'm full now. Then he let go of me.

Okay, this was just so weird.

"I wonder how long I can stay here. I really like it here and would like to wait until my week is up. Is that okay with you, little man?"

Yes, because I see Daddy in my dreams.

My mind started to go around and around. I heard that before, but where? I knew of this. I looked down at the little man with my eyes wide.

Yes, he said he was going to see you next, and then he was gone. But he held me and fed me also. Hugged me tight and gave lots of kisses.

"I love you, Bryan."

He smiled up at me and fell back asleep. That was the weirdest thing I had ever been through. I so did not get what was going on with my mind. I placed him back into his basket and kissed his forehead. Then I climbed back into bed and hoped I would have a peaceful night of sleep.

When I woke up the next day, I just stood staring at Bryan. Was what happened real? Maybe I slept through it, and it was just another dream. I walked off and got ready for the day before he woke up. I could hear his crying from the kitchen, making me turn off the stove and go get him. I picked him up and looked into his eyes. There was nothing there like last night. Maybe it was a dream. I got him changed and fed before going back to the kitchen, holding him to make my breakfast again. When I was done, I set Bryan down and ate my food. Mike came in a little after that, ready for coffee.

"There is fresh coffee in the pot. I made it just for you."

"Thanks, Willow. How was your night?"

"Well, to tell the truth, it was messed up." I looked over at Bryan, and I swear he winked at me.

"Oh? So what happened?"

"Well, Asher dream-walked into my dream. He explained to me that he was under a spell, and that is why he said all those things to Violet. She wanted us to be apart and not raise our kid together. Then he left, and I was still in the same field, and the Moon goddess came and talked to me about Bryan. She gave me several choices as to what to do with my life. Then Bryan woke up, and I swear he was talking to me in my mind. Now, I have no clue if I was awake for feeding Bryan or not. It could have just been a dream also. So I am not well rested this morning."

It was not a dream, but Mike cannot know about it being real. He will kill me.

I looked over to Bryan with wide eyes. What was he talking about? I thought, if he could talk to me in my head, maybe I could talk to him also. But before I could talk to him, Mike started to talk.

"What do you mean talking to you?"

I looked over at Bryan again before I opened my mouth.

"Oh, it is nothing. Just another dream. No kid can talk like that until they find their wolf, and at one week old, there is no way Bryan has found his. It was just part of the dream. If it were real, he would be talking this morning, and he is not."

I will not tell him, I promise. I looked at Bryan, and he smiled at me.

So he could hear me the same way.

"Well, if you say so. But keep an eye out for anything weird that he does."

"Why should I do that? He is just a kid, Mike."

"I know, but you never know who someone is and what they can do."

I nodded my head and went back to eating my breakfast. After I was done, I walked over to pick up Bryan.

"I think I am going to go for a little walk in the woods. I will be back soon. Bye, Mike."

"Bye, and be safe. I am going to town to get some food. We are almost out."

I waved and walked out the door.

He is following us.

I know, Bryan. Just give me a second, and I will call him out on it.

I walked a little bit more before I turned around.

"Is there a reason you are following me, Mike?"

"No, I just wanted to make sure you are okay."

"Go do your shopping. Bryan and I are okay."

I watched him leave before I started to run. I ran for a little bit before I stopped and sat down. I turned my ears up to see if I could hear anything. There were only birds and nature making noise. I looked down at Bryan in my arms and pulled him close to me in a hug.

He is gone now. Can I show you something?

I nodded my head at Bryan, and he started to change. His bones where popping and snapping. I laid him down on the ground and watched him become a little pup. He was all black except for his paws which were white and the tips of his ears and tail. I smiled at him.

"You look like you are wearing socks. That is just too cute."

I stood up and changed into a wolf form. Man, it felt good to shift again. Ruth shook out her fur and stretched. The little pup started to bark at Ruth.

Hello, my son, Ruth said as she snuggled up to the pup.

Both of us could hear the pup purring.

Momma, I do not have a name. Will you name me?

I am going to call you Socks. That is just for us. But your big-wolf name will be Zander.

I like that a lot. Thank you.

Ruth and Socks lay there just enjoying the sun and being together. It felt like hours before Socks spoke up.

Momma, Mike is coming. We need to change back.

Bryan started to snap and pop and changed back to his human form. He lay there and pulled on his diaper, and I just raised an eyebrow at him.

Yeah, I can do a lot of things that you have no idea of. But stay as your wolf, and I will lie with you. Bryan moved to where he was lying beside me again.

I moved to be closer to him and pulled him into me. I heard a snap of a branch and knew it was Mike but still jumped up over Bryan to protect him.

Mike came out from the trees holding his hands up. "It is just me, Ruth. I am not going to hurt your pup. I figured you went for a run and needed a change of clothes. I will hold Bryan while you change."

I growled at him, not leaving the pup.

"Okay, I get it. I will just leave these here. I will see you back at the house." Mike turned and walked away.

I shifted back into my human form and put the clothes on. I picked up Bryan and walked back to the house. I had to go back to Asher, but I did not think that Mike would let me go.

Asher, can you hear me? I kept walking, waiting to see if he could hear me.

Yes, but I cannot talk here. I will talk to you again like last night. Just wait for me.

I nodded my head and kept walking to the house. When I got there, I placed Bryan into his basket, and Mike started to ask about my day. I told him that I just went for a run and let Ruth met her new pup. After that, Bryan and I went into my room for the rest of the day. I had got to get us out of here. We were not safe here.

CHAPTER

Dream.

I woke up in a green field filled with high green grass and wild-flowers. I looked around to see if I was alone or anyone was around.

"Asher? Are you here?" I asked, looking around.

I saw something move from over by the trees to the left. Slowly Asher came walking out of the woods. I got up and walked to Asher, wrapping my arms around his neck.

"I am so sorry, Asher. I am ready to come home, but I cannot."

"Why can you not come home? I have made everything for you guys. Please come back."

"Asher, I want to. Believe me, I want to. But Mike…he will not let me. I had no clue that he was an evil person and that he had a plan when he asked me to come with. Bryan told me that he cannot be trusted and that he is here to kill Bryan."

"What do you mean 'Bryan told you'?"

"Bryan is a special pup. He already has a wolf named Socks and, as an adult wolf, named Zander. Ruth named the adult wolf. I named the pup wolf. He is pure black besides his paws and tip of ears, and tail is white. They look like socks. He can talk to me through the mind-link. He is so strong already. The Moon Goddess came to me and told me that he is going to be strong and mighty, that he will be important in the wolf world, to be careful because people will seek to destroy him. Mike is that person."

"Tell me where you are, and I will come get you."

"We are on an island in the middle of nowhere. We are in a small cabin up in the hills. There is a waterfall close by. It is named

Life Well. It is a place where people who are feeling sick go and get their strength from. We are one hour to the southwest from the top of the waterfall. Mike keeps us locked up inside now that I have shifted. I turned into a wolf, and Mike saw me like that. He had locked the door to where I cannot get out. I have Bryan with me. I even lock my door and him in the bathroom with me when I shower. Asher, please come for us soon. I am trying to stay strong for Bryan, but Mike is trying to tear me down."

"I will come as fast as I can come. Please, hold on for both of us. We need you."

I reached up and kissed Asher. I nodded my head and hugged him tight to me. I could not let this feeling go. I refused to lose my mate, the father of my pup. I opened my eyes, and I was sitting on a river side next to the Moon Goddess.

"Hello, Willow."

"Hello."

"I have come to see what you want to do. Have you made up your mind already? You still have four days."

"I have already made up my mind. I want Asher. I want a life with him. I want to be with him as a mate. I want to keep all my memories because they will make me stronger. I choose this life with him."

"As you wish. I will make it easy for you. I grant little Bryan the ability to shape-shift also for the next five days. All you must do is tell him what animal to be, and his little body will change into it. Maybe that will help in you guys getting free and finding Asher."

"Thank you."

I woke up in my own bed again covered in sweat. I walked over to Bryan and looked down at him. He smiled up at me and winked. Silly pup.

Cat. I said in his head.

He shifted and became a cat. There were no bones popping or snapping. There was just a cat there. I blinked once, twice, and a third time.

Bryan.

And right before my eyes was my little guy. He smiled up at me, and I just could not believe my eyes. My son was a shape-shifter. I could get us out of here and maybe fly us back to Asher. I could save us. My mind went back to Asher. Would we miss each other if I left after breakfast? While I was thinking that, the door opened, and in walked Mike. I picked up Bryan and went to change his diaper.

"I got breakfast for you, Willow."

"Why in here?"

"I thought you could use a day of rest after changing into your wolf after such a long time. I figured you would be tired. How about I take Bryan for the day, and you just rest?"

"No, that is okay. I have to feed him several times a day, or he screams without his mom."

"I have never heard him do that before. Here, let me take him."

As he reached for Bryan, he let out a bloodcurdling scream. Mike slammed his hands over his ears. I pulled Bryan closer to me and shushed him. Bryan quieted down, and Mike reached for him again. And once again, Bryan screamed. Mike backed up with his hands in the air.

"Okay, okay, okay. I get the point. I am going to the store again today. I will see you later today." He turned and walked out the door after that.

I sat down on the bed and laid Bryan next to me.

Asher, you care for a nap?

When I did not hear anything, I lay back down on the bed. Slowly I closed my eyes and went to sleep.

Dream.

"Willow, are you here?"

"I am here!"

"What is going on?"

I took in a deep breath and spoke as fast as I could, "The Moon Goddess came to me after you left last night. She has given Bryan the ability to shape-shift for several days. I can get us out of here as spiders, then change him into a bug that will hold onto my bird and fly home to you."

Asher smiled from ear to ear. "Do you think it will work?"

"Yes, I already tried it on him. I say the animal in his head, and he changes. Then I say his name, and he changes back to his human form. I can get us out of here."

"Do it. Come home. I will wait for you."

"I love you, Asher."

"I love you, Willow."

I woke up and looked down at Bryan. He was smiling up at me. I smiled and said, "Let's get home to Dad."

He clapped and giggled.

Spider.

Bryan shifted into a baby spider and I into a bigger one. Bryan climbed onto my back, and I climbed up high onto the walls.

Hold on tight, little one. We are going home.

Yes, Momma.

I climbed up and out of the house, not looking back once. Once we were far enough from the cabin, I changed back into a human and looked down at the spider in my hand.

"I am going to change into a bird. I will need you to climb onto me and hold on tight. Can you do that for me?"

Yes, Momma. Let us go get Daddy.

I changed into a bird, and Bryan climbed up onto my back. I took off flying toward our home. Toward Asher.

CHAPTER

Every night, we would stop and sleep in a tree. I would say his name after I changed to a human form. We would sleep up in the treetops. He would feed from me, and I would eat what was in the trees. I would sleep for a little bit before I changed him back to a spider and me a bird and took off again. It was on day four when I finally made it back to the pack line. I lowered myself to the ground and looked around for some clothes in the trees. I found some shorts and a shirt. It smelled like Asher, so I put them on. The shorts were way too big, so I used them to wrap Bryan up in. I leaned down and said in his head for him to change back into a human. After he was back to human, I wrapped him in the shorts. I looked up at the pack line and took one step over it. I heard growls coming at me, and I just stood still. Three wolves came charging at me, but when they saw I was not moving, they slowed down. One wolf stayed in front of me, growling, and the other two left to change and get dressed. They brought another pair of shorts with them. The one wolf then changed in front of me and pulled the shorts on.

"Who are you, and what are you doing here on our land?" Jason growled at me.

I smiled up at him.

"Willow, is that you?"

"Yes, it is me, and this is Asher's son, Bryan. Can we see Asher now?"

He nodded his head, and we started to follow him.

"Where have you been? When Asher came back without your or Bryan, I was afraid something bad happened to you."

"It did. Asher was under a spell, and so was I. But now we are better and can be joined again."

We got to the pack house, and I heard a howl go out from the house. Loud steps could be heard outside while there was running happening. Asher made it out the door in a flash, and I was swept up into his arms in a tight hug.

"Asher, I am afraid that Bryan cannot breathe between us."

Asher let go and looked down at his son. Bryan reached up for his dad with his small arms. Asher looked at me with a question, and I nodded at him. Asher got Bryan from my arms and hugged him to his chest. He looked up at me and took my hand, leading me inside. He dragged me up the stairs and into his office. The room looked just the same as last time. He set us down on the couch and pulled me close to him.

"How many more days until he can no longer shape-shift?"

"Tonight at midnight is when it is done."

"Can you have him change into something?"

I smiled up at Asher and shook my head no. Asher started to pout at me when I let out a little chuckle.

"You can do it yourself. You tell him what animal you want, and he changes."

"Rabbit."

Nothing happened.

"Try it through mind-link."

It was quiet for a little bit, and suddenly there was a rabbit in Asher's arms. He smiled up at me and then looked back at Bryan. He rubbed his fur before changing him back to his human form.

"I would like to see his wolf."

"I am not sure how he does that one. I think we should wait until tomorrow when the shape-shifter part is gone."

"I get that. I am so glad you guys are here safe and sound."

"Have you told anyone about Mike? Will he be able to get to us?"

"Willow, you are safe here. Mike will be taken to the basement if he shows back up here again. You do not take the Luna away without something getting done. He will not get near you."

"Thank you."

Asher held me for what felt like hours before Bryan wanted to feed. So I got up and walked to his room to grab a diaper and change him. After that was done, I sat down in a chair and fed him. I placed him in is basket and took it to the bedroom I was staying in.

"Here, little guy, this is our new room for now."

I set him down on the bed in his basket and walked back to the door to close it. Asher was standing out in the hall watching us with glazed eyes.

"Asher, are you okay?"

"No, I am not. Can I please stay with you guys tonight? I will even grab his crib and place it in here. I do not want to be away from you."

"Yes, you can stay. Please grab the crib. I cannot sleep without him right now. I need to feel my baby close to me."

He nodded his head and walked out of the room.

"What am I going to do with your silly father?"

Love him and me. That is all that matters.

I smiled down at Bryan and pulled him out of the basket and hugged him.

"I do love both of you so much."

Asher walked back in at that time and placed the crib by the window.

"No, not there. Over here by me please. I need to be able to see him in the dark."

Asher nodded at me and moved the crib over to my side of the bed. We placed Bryan in it together and just stood and watched him.

"Good night, my son," Asher said.

His eyes hazed over, so I am sure that Bryan was talking back to him. He looked up at me and smiled from ear to ear.

"That is so cool. I am not ever getting used to it."

I patted him on the back and walked to the bathroom.

I took a quick shower and put on new shorts and shirt and walked back out. Asher was lying in bed without a shirt on. I knew I had drool rolling out of my mouth. Asher winked at me and patted the bed for me to join him. I walked over and climbed into bed with Asher pulling me closer to him.

"Good night, my mate. I will never let you go again," Asher whispered in my ear.

"Good night," I said sleepily.

I closed my eyes, and that was the last I remember of that day.

EPILOGUE

Three weeks have passed since I came back home. Bryan keeps on growing fast. Asher has stepped up and shown me how he is so sorry for everything. I keep up with my boys and watch them grow, both in size and in mind. One of these days, Bryan will rule over the were-wolves. One of these days, I will be gone and only dream of being with my family again. I hope I have a long life with my guys. I hope we have another pup. Mike has not shown up yet. I am waiting for that day to come. Someone from somewhere will show up for my pup. I just hope we are all ready for it when it happens. Maybe one day, we will look back and see nothing but love and life. The only thing I can do now is live each day as my last.

ABOUT THE AUTHOR

Erica is the mother of four girls and a wife of over twenty years and counting. She has been a stay-at-home mom since her first girl was born. She has had to deal with health issues and wakes up every day thankful for the life she was given. She loves photography and painting landscapes in her free time. She has read every book in her library.